Karen woke [ ] h a
start. The [ ] he
Fairgates ha[ ]d to
be stopped. Her lies were destroying Sid
and everything he had worked so hard to
build. Slowly Karen forced her mind into
focus. This was no time for rash action. She
had to come up with a plan. Suddenly, she
knew just what to do.

Series Story Editor **Mary Ann Cooper** is
America's foremost soap opera expert. She
writes the nationally syndicated column
Speaking of Soaps, is a major contributor to
soap opera magazines and has appeared on
numerous radio and television talk shows.

Scott Cunningham, author of *Tell Me No
Lies*, is an experienced screen writer who
currently resides in California.

Dear Friend,

One of the nicest things about serving as Story Editor for Soaps & Serials books is the opportunity to read the wonderful letters I receive from our readers. It's gratifying to know how much you enjoy these books. At Pioneer we work with the finest romance authors and editors to produce books that recapture, relish, and relive the rich history of soap operas through the retelling of stories that have entertained millions of viewers over the years.

These books bring back precious memories of the past, but they raise questions, too. A reader from Encino, California, wrote to inquire about the actor who plays Gary Ewing in KNOTS LANDING. She recalled a very different looking actor playing the part in the original pilot of DALLAS, the show that gave birth to some of our favorite characters from KNOTS LANDING. Although Ted Shackelford has portrayed Gary Ewing through the course of the series, an actor named John Ackroyd originated the role. We'll answer other reader questions in future books.

For Soaps & Serials Books,

Mary Ann Cooper

Mary Ann Cooper

P.S. If you missed previous volumes of Soaps & Serials books and can't find them in your local book source, please see the order form inserted in this book.

KNOTS LANDING

7

Tell Me No Lies

From the television series created by David Jacobs

PIONEER COMMUNICATIONS NETWORK, INC.

Tell Me No Lies

From the television series KNOTS LANDING™
created by David Jacobs. This book is based on
scripts written by Don Murray.

KNOTS LANDING™ paperback novels are
published and distributed by Pioneer
Communications Network, Inc.

SOAPS & SERIALS™ is a trademark of Pioneer
Communications Network, Inc.

ISBN: 0-916217-67-1

Printed in Canada

10 9 8 7 6 5 4 3 2 1

Tell Me No Lies

Chapter One

Sid's Nightmare

"Mother, hurry!" Diana Fairgate yelled as she bounded down the stairs, dressed in sweat pants and a T-shirt.

"We've got plenty of time, Diana," Karen Fairgate called from upstairs.

"But it's almost five-thirty!" Diana told her anxiously. She glanced in a mirror, running her hands through her short, curly brown hair.

"The talent show doesn't start until seven-thirty, and you don't go on until eight. There's no big rush, honey."

The sixteen-year-old scowled at her reflection. "Easy for you to say. You don't go on stage tonight. I just *know* I'm gonna blow it. I'll forget a word, drop my cane or step on Cindy's foot."

"You'll be fine," Karen said as she descended the stairs. She looked beautiful in her simple black dress, a soft white sweater

7

draped over her shoulders. Her wavy black hair framed her face, highlighting the radiant beauty of her features.

"I just hope Daddy'll be there. I can't *believe* he had to drive to San Luis Obispo today!"

"He didn't have any choice, sweetheart," Karen said with a smile. "You know your Aunt Abby's moving out of her house today, since the divorce was finalized. She can't do it all by herself with two kids underfoot—she really needed your father's help. There are some things that brothers and sisters just have to do for each other." Karen's voice trailed off and she shrugged.

"You and Aunt Abby don't like each other, do you?" Diana asked quietly.

"That's not true," her mother said with little conviction. "We sometimes have arguments, but that's because we don't always see things the same way." Diana, she decided, was growing shrewder by the minute.

"But why'd she have to move out today?" Diana whined.

Karen folded her arms across her chest and studied her daughter. "Twist of fate, kiddo. But try not to worry. And by the way, Diana, you look beautiful."

In spite of herself, Diana smiled. "Really?" She turned back to the mirror. Even she had to admit that she looked pretty. Her hair was just right and excitement had brought a delightful flush to her cheeks.

But her smile faded as she continued to stare into the mirror. "I hope he makes it, Mom."

Karen hesitated for a brief moment, unable to hide her frustration. "San Luis Obispo's a long way away," she reminded her gently. "But I hope so, too."

Diana turned away from the mirror. Disappointment was etched on her pretty face. "Eric and Michael are already waiting outside. Let's go."

"Okay," Karen said quietly. "Please don't worry, Diana—"she started to say, but her daughter had already left the house.

Sid Fairgate passed yet another car on the crowded freeway. The traffic was terrible, but at last he was nearing Knots Landing.

He checked his speedometer and was surprised to see that he was speeding. He glanced at his watch. Seven-ten. He might still make it in time.

In the long run, the Knots Landing High School Follies wouldn't be the most important event in his life—or Diana's—but tonight it was everything.

Sid had heard of little else over the last two weeks. His house had seen endless costume fittings and rehearsals. He'd listened to the same songs being sung over and over, and heard the patter of feet as his daughter practiced her dance steps in her bedroom.

And then, the night before the big performance, Abby had called, pleading for

9

his help. She was moving to San Diego.

Sid shrugged with good-natured resignation. Abby had a way of getting just about anything she wanted. And why she'd wanted him to be there, Sid couldn't imagine. All day she hadn't needed his help, but she kept insisting that he stick around "just in case."

He checked his watch again and gently increased the pressure on the gas pedal. Three more exits and he'd be off the freeway.

"I'll make it," he murmured. "With or without Abby's interference, I'll see Diana in her show tonight."

"I love your purple face," Diana said to her companion as they stood backstage at Knots Landing High School.

"Thanks." Kevin touched his cheek gingerly. "It took me two hours to put it on. The silver around the eyes was the hardest."

Diana nodded, gazing at him. "Anything for show business, right?"

"No, just music." Kevin was tall and lean, dressed in fake leather and plastic studs. His hair stood straight up in spikes, thickly coated with petroleum jelly.

Diana's eyes shone as she stared at him. "You look great, Kevin. You really do."

He shot her a knowing look, ready with a smart comeback. But then he smiled. "So do you," he said quietly, letting his eyes move over her slender form.

Diana's cheeks burned. "I—I mean, your

look," she stammered. "It's so authentic."

"Thanks," he said. "I looked at a picture of a heavy metal band for days, trying to match it perfectly. Well, not quite. I did my own customizing."

Not far from them on the stage, a teen-aged Houdini produced a bouquet of flaming flowers from a pitcher of milk. The audience applauded enthusiastically.

The magician motioned toward his young assistant, a blond beauty who stood quivering by the curtain.

Just then, a spark flew off the burning flowers and landed on the stage. The assistant watched in horror as the magician ran toward a metal trash can with the blazing flowers in his hand. He stumbled, sending a shower of sparks dancing across the stage.

"Oh my—" Karen began, then shot past a couple rehearsing in the wings. She pulled the fire extinguisher from its hook beside the light board and strode toward the stage. "Close the curtains!" she yelled, aiming the fire extinguisher at the flowers. A stream of chemical smoke filled the air.

The audience applauded vigorously as the curtain dropped.

Backstage, a second curtain rose, revealing the set for the next performance. Unaware of the commotion all around them, Kevin and Diana stood by the band equipment. They were holding hands.

"Hey, way to go, Kevin!" a male voice boomed out of the wings. "She's some hot babe!" Several crew members whistled.

Diana dropped her hand, smiling shyly. "I'll see you later," she whispered to Kevin. "Good luck!"

Four other boys, dressed in outlandish costumes and makeup, joined Kevin on stage. Amplifier lights snapped on and the band tuned their instruments. Nervous electricity crackled in the air.

"And now," the announcer's voice boomed, "Zarris!"

As the curtain opened, the band came to life. Jumping around to the deafening music, the boys began to rock the auditorium. Playing a mean guitar, Kevin raced his fingers over the strings.

"Yeah!" Diana yelled from the wings as she watched Kevin perform. "You're doing great!"

Not far off, Karen stood smiling at her daughter, her face filled with pride. It was almost time for Diana to go on. Karen glanced out into the audience, letting her eyes move over the familiar faces there. She saw Val Ewing, Ginger Ward, and her two sons, Eric and Michael.

Sid was nowhere in sight.

Sid drove down the broad thoroughfare six miles from Knots Landing High School. The street was deserted, since it was long past rush hour. He frowned as he glanced at his watch. It was going to be close.

Stopping at a red light, Sid looked out his

side window and saw that the cross street was empty, except for an orange van at the corner. The van's engine was running, but it made no attempt to move when the light changed to green.

"Hi," a voice suddenly came out of the darkness.

Sid turned quickly. A pretty young blonde was leaning through his car window, smiling hopefully at him. She blew a bubble with her gum. "Can you give me a ride?"

Sid shook his head. "Sorry. I'm in a real hurry."

"Oh come on," she pleaded. "*I'm* in a hurry too, and it's not safe out here. Just give me a lift."

"Hitchhiking isn't safe either," Sid said. "You shouldn't be out here at this time of night."

"You want me off the streets? Then give me a ride, mister. Come on!" The girl tried the door handle but it was locked.

"Sorry," Sid said with a frown, pressing a button to close the front window.

"Thanks a lot," she snapped as the window closed shut.

As the girl stepped back from the car, the orange van suddenly pulled up beside her.

"Hey, hot stuff!" one of the men from the van called.

Sid looked over at the girl, who stood forlornly on the sidewalk.

"Forget it, loser," she shouted, then turned and walked away.

Sid drove slowly through the intersection, then pulled over to the curb on the other side. He twisted to look over his shoulder.

The blond girl stood twenty feet from the van. A man jumped out and walked up to her. Then he grabbed the girl's wrist.

"Hey, stop it!" she cried out.

Sid shifted into reverse and gunned his motor. His car shot back with a squeal, and he began pounding on the horn. The attacker looked up in surprise, and released the girl's arm. Sid's car halted beside the pair.

"Get in!" he yelled, unlocking the door.

The girl hesitated for a moment, then opened the door and slid in. "Thanks," she said, popping her bubble gum.

"That was close," Sid said, curious at the girl's lack of fear.

"Sure," she said carelessly. "You got a cigarette?"

"No, I don't smoke."

"Oh. Neither do I." She smiled coyly at Sid.

He reached in front of her to lock her door. The girl pressed herself back against the seat cushions, eyeing him flirtatiously. "Hey, you're not getting fresh, are you?"

Sid laughed. There was something strange about the girl. After the episode with the van, she shouldn't be joking around. "No. I just don't want something like that to happen again. You okay?"

She shrugged. "Sure."

"You don't seem very shook up."

"Happens all the time, mister. A guy gets drunk or stoned, sees me, decides he wants to . . . you know." She cast him a knowing look. "Thanks for saving me."

"Any time." He drove on toward the school and glanced in his rearview mirror. The orange van was following him at a distance. Sid stepped on the gas.

"I'm Pam," the blonde said, popping a bubble.

"Sid Fairgate. Where are you headed?"

"Clear across the city. And you?" She looked at him quizzically, then glanced over her shoulder.

"The high school."

"That's fine with me."

"Good." Sid smiled warily. He wasn't sure what to make of this girl. "I'm going to see my daughter perform in the Knots Landing Follies."

"*Follies?*" Pam asked disdainfully.

"Yeah, follies. Talent show. You know."

"Oh, right," she said.

"If you don't mind my asking, aren't you afraid to hitchhike?"

"I have to get around somehow, and I'm not rich. I don't have a car."

"There are buses," Sid pointed out.

Pam shrugged. "They don't go where I go."

"Really? So guys like those ones in that van back there don't bother you? You're not scared?"

"Hey, Sid, for every one of them, there's

one like you—a hero." She smiled slowly, letting her eyes linger on the handsome man beside her.

Zarris' performance built to a shuddering conclusion with an assault of electric music and an explosion of special effects.

"The crowd loves them!" Diana said, grabbing her mother's arm as they watched the band from offstage.

"It seems they do," Karen agreed. She looked out at the audience and saw their enthusiasm. As the band started to leave the stage, Karen called out to Kevin.

The boy turned, his face slick with sweat. "What?" he panted.

"Go ahead and do another one. They really like you!" Karen said.

Kevin gave her a "thumbs up" sign and the band geared up for the next song. As they performed, Karen pulled back the curtain to look at the audience again. Though Val, Ginger, and her sons seemed to be enjoying the show, they were still alone—Sid hadn't shown up yet.

"Do you see Daddy out there?" Diana asked.

Karen quickly closed the curtains and turned to her daughter. "No, not yet, but he'll probably be here any second."

Diana frowned. "You don't sound too sure of that."

Karen looked at her daughter. She was dressed in her costume—a glittery white coat, black leotard, white satin bow tie, and black mesh stockings. She looked so pretty, so eager . . . if only Sid were here to see her!

"Well, I'm glad *you* could make it," Diana said, trying to sound cheerful.

Karen gave her a hug of support, then took up her position at the curtain, staring out at the empty seat beside Eric. It was getting so close to Diana's performance. She couldn't delay it any longer with the band.

Where on earth was Sid?

"Sid, can I ask you a question?"

"Sure," he answered. They were six blocks from the school.

"Do you know how much money you have in your wallet right now?" Pam asked sweetly.

"No," he said with a chuckle. "Haven't counted it lately. Why?"

"I have mysterious powers," she said, snapping her gum. "I'm psychic. Let me tell you. A hundred, right?" She looked at him eagerly.

"Maybe. Probably less."

She smiled. "Give it to me." Her voice was soft, but steady.

Sid laughed. So she wanted to play games. "No."

"Please?" she pleaded. "I need it to go home to visit my parents. They're really sick."

"Really? I'll drive you to the bus station after the Follies."

"Give it to me, Sid. Give me the hundred." She looked at him intently and ran her tongue over her lips.

"Sorry, Pam." He frowned. What was this girl up to?

"If you don't give it to me, Sid, I'll scream rape. I'm serious."

He laughed. "Sure. Look, it's safe here. Maybe I should let you out?"

"I'm not joking. I mean it." Her voice was breathy with exasperation. "Seventy-five. Okay? Give me seventy-five and I won't scream."

Sid pulled up to a stop light and saw a police car parked outside an all-night donut shop across the intersection. "I don't buy it," Sid said. "If you were going to scream rape, you'd do it now."

"Why?" Pam asked, confused by the unexpected turn of events.

"There's a cop car right over there," Sid said, pointing to it.

Pam hadn't noticed the car. Her eyes flashed as she saw the black and white. She looked at Sid, then back at the police car. "All right, have it your way," she murmured angrily. Grabbing hold of her sleeve, she ripped the fragile material of her blouse.

"What are you—" Sid began.

Pam opened her window. "Rape! Rape!" she screamed. She slammed her foot down on the gas pedal and twisted the steering wheel, sending the car wildly through the intersection.

As Sid tried to regain control, Pam pounded on the horn. He pushed her foot off the gas, stepped on the brake, and began fighting off her blows.

The police were on the street, steaming coffee and cinnamon rolls forgotten, by the time Sid's car came to a stop.

"All right, all right," one of the cops said, as he ran up to the car. "What's going on here?"

Sid tried to twist out of the girl's grip as the policeman threw the car door open and pulled Sid out. Pam continued to scream as she was helped from the car by the second officer. When her feet hit the street she collapsed into the young man's arms, clinging to him.

"I'm Officer Thompson," the first cop said. "Okay, buddy, spread your legs, put your hands on the car roof. Come on, let's go," he ordered.

Sid assumed the position, his mind spinning. "Wait a minute—this is a mistake!" he cried.

"Sure, and you made it, buddy," the cop said.

A van—the same one he'd seen earlier—sped by the scene, clanking as it hit a pothole. Sid looked up and saw it pass.

"He tried to *rape* me!" Pam screamed with sudden passion. "He tried—"

"Okay, calm down, miss," the officer said as she cried hysterically in his arms.

Sid shook his head. "Officer, it's not like

that at all—" he began.

"Maybe you'd better not say anything right now, Mr. Fairgate," the policeman said. "Not until you speak with your lawyer."

Sid let his head fall against the car roof and felt the first cold twinge of fear chill him. His arms were pulled roughly behind him and steel handcuffs clicked around his wrists.

Sorry, Diana, he thought bitterly. *I won't make it to your performance tonight.*

Karen watched proudly as Diana and her two friends sang and danced their way through the intricate musical number. With top hats and canes, the three teenagers from Knots Landing created a moment of Broadway razzle-dazzle.

Karen held her hands to her mouth, smiling in wonder at her daughter's talent. But half-way through the number, Karen saw Diana turn to search the seats for her father.

Karen's smile faded, then died completely. The seat beside her son in the audience was still empty. Sid had missed Diana's performance.

She tried to fight the fear that suddenly gripped her. But she knew in her heart that something was dreadfully wrong.

Sid was in trouble.

Chapter Two

Beyond Belief

The round-faced, balding newspaperman leaned against the wall, slurping his diet soft drink. He stared into a large metal cage that sat in the inspector's room at the Knots Landing Police Station.

Sid leaned forward on the bench inside the holding cell. As he glanced up at the clock that hung over the door he noticed the journalist's stare.

"You got a problem?" Sid asked.

The man flashed a false smile. "Looks like you're the one with the problem, fella."

"Les Carney, you old yellow journalist. What're you doing here?" an authoritative man in a gray suit asked as he strode into the room.

"Lieutenant Spatz," the fat reporter said with a smile. "I'm just getting some good copy."

"And pictures," a pale, skinny man said

from a chair by the pay phone. He held up his camera.

"What made you think you'd get anything tonight?" Spatz asked, frowning.

"You know, Spatz, sometimes I get this feeling," Carney said. "And look who dropped in to pay you a visit."

The lieutenant looked into the cage and suddenly froze. "Sid?"

Sid gazed up at him. "Hi, Walter."

"You sure are a surprise. I never thought I'd see you in there. How'd this happen? What's going on here?"

Sid laughed nervously. "You tell me. I feel ridiculous," he said, standing. Maybe now that Walter had come, he could be finished with this mess and get to the talent show—if it hadn't already ended.

Walter Spatz glanced around the room. A blond teenager was flirting with Officer Bright. Officer Thompson was typing up a report.

"What's that?" Walter asked, walking to the cop's desk. He leaned over to read the report. Walter frowned and turned to the girl. "Is this what happened, Miss Messinger?"

"Of course," Pam said. "You don't think I'd lie about something like this, do you?" she asked innocently, her voice filled with emotion.

Spatz turned to the officer. "Thompson, has Fairgate made his call yet?"

"No, sir," the uniform replied.

Walter nodded and walked to the holding

pen. Pulling a key from his pocket, he unlocked the door. A bemused Sid emerged, stretching his legs.

"We need to talk, Sid," Spatz said, patting the man gently on the shoulder. The lieutenant led Fairgate to his office, a partitioned corner of the huge room.

Sid sat awkwardly on the chair before Lt. Walter Spatz's desk. The man sighed as he stared at Sid.

"What in the hell is going on here?" the lieutenant asked.

Sid frowned. "Walter, I wish I knew."

Laura Avery entered the bedroom wearing a luxurious nightgown of peach silk and delicate lace. "I'm so tired," she said as she approached the bed.

"Work hard today?" Richard asked smugly, arms crossed on his hairy chest. He stared at his wife.

"Yes, I did," Laura said quietly. She slid between the flowered sheets beside him.

"What'd you do at Scooter's real estate office? Work the Xerox machine?"

She tried to ignore the sarcastic comment. "I like working, Richard. As hard as that may be for you to believe."

"What's there to like about it? You can lick stamps and stuff envelopes at home, honey." He scratched his chin and yawned loudly.

"I enjoy working around other people, keeping busy all day," Laura said, too tired to fight. "It's exciting being in real estate."

"You're only a secretary," Richard pointed out disparagingly.

"I'm enjoying it and feeling my way around the business. It's a beginning, and that's good enough for me."

Richard sighed dramatically. "You really shouldn't set your goals so high, Laura," he drawled.

Laura's temper flared. Why did she put up with him? Day after day, night after night, their loveless marriage was more a competition than a relationship. Angry, she switched off the bedside light to avoid another confrontation.

The phone rang. Richard groaned and answered it. "Hello?" he said. "Yeah, hello, Sid. How are—" He was silent for a moment. "What?" He lifted his eyebrows in shock. "I can't believe it. No, relax, I'll be right over. Yeah. I'll have Karen tag along with me. Just relax, Sid. Don't talk to anyone! I'm on my way!" Richard slammed down the phone, jumped up from bed, and hastily grabbed his pants.

"What is it, Richard?" Laura asked. "Is Sid in some kind of trouble?"

"Trouble? Sid's in jail," he said, throwing open the closet doors.

"What?"

He dressed quickly, then took his keys and wallet from the dresser. "Some hitchhiker Sid picked up tonight accused him of attempted rape." He paused. "She's only seventeen."

Laura's hand flew to her mouth in shock. "I'm going with you!"

"No. Stay here with Jason, and call Val to go over and help with Karen and Sid's kids," he ordered.

Laura bent her head in resignation. "All right, Richard."

Richard didn't look back as he stormed out the bedroom door.

"Since you're an established local resident, Sid, I can release you on your own recognizance," Lt. Spatz said, peering out from behind his office window blinds to the room beyond.

Sid sat beside his wife and Richard Avery. The three of them watched the policeman intently.

"But after that?" Karen asked, trying to hide the quaver in her voice.

But the lieutenant was interested in something in the station room and didn't hear the question.

Karen realized that his attention was elsewhere. Rising quickly from her seat, she joined Spatz and peered out into the other room.

Looking refreshed and at ease, Pam Messinger sat at an officer's desk, flirting outrageously with a handsome policeman. She smiled at something he said, then laughed raucously.

Karen turned to the lieutenant and pointed to Pam. "Look at her! Does she look like a girl who's just been assaulted?"

Spatz smiled. "She's enjoying all the trouble she's causing, no doubt about that. But I'm sure the District Attorney won't buy her story."

"Why not?" Sid asked. "I know she's lying, but how will the D.A.?"

"She isn't reliable. Besides, I seriously doubt she'll show up for the preliminary hearing." He let the window blinds drop back into place.

"When's that?" Sid asked.

"Tuesday. But she'll probably disappear on us."

"Is there a chance of that?" Karen asked hopefully.

"It's possible. But even if she *does* show, you're pretty safe, Sid. With your reputation her case doesn't stand a chance. Besides, what's in it for her?" Spatz smiled confidently.

"I just wish I could get out of bed in the morning and find this whole thing was a dream."

"Nightmare, you mean," Karen said, and rubbed her husband's shoulders. "I hope you're right, Walter."

"I'm sure he is," Richard said.

Spatz picked up a folded document from his desk and handed it to Avery. "The summons," he explained.

Karen stared at it blankly. "Summons?"

"We have to go through the motions, Karen," Lt. Spatz said with a helpless shrug.

26

"Now why don't you all just go home. Forget about it until Tuesday."

"Thanks, Walter," Sid said, smiling bravely.

Richard pumped the lieutenant's hand. "We appreciate it."

The three of them started to leave the office.

"Wait a minute!" Pam Messinger cried as she saw Sid appear from the room. "Where's he going? He can't just walk out of here. He should be locked up—for good!" She pouted, slid off the desk and pointed an accusing finger at Sid.

Spatz came out of his office. "He's been released on his own recognizance to his lawyer," he told her.

"But he can't be!" Pam said angrily. "That man almost raped me!"

"Let's split," Richard muttered, gently taking hold of Karen's arm.

"Come on, honey," Sid said.

But Karen stood frozen, staring at the girl.

"You got a minute, Mrs. Fairgate?" Pam asked bitterly, sneering at the well-dressed woman. "You wanna hear a few things about your *respectable* husband?"

"That's enough," Richard snapped.

"Come on!" Sid said. "Let's get out of here."

"Oh, sure, try to make a clean break. You'll be flying off to Rio by morning!" Pam yelled.

Carney, the newspaperman, and his photographer sidekick walked closer to the

27

scene as Pam followed the departing trio.

"Your husband tricked me into his car, Mrs. Fairgate, describing all the horrible things those guys in the van would do to me. Then once he had me locked in his car, he said he'd pay me to have sex with him. He even took a hundred dollars out of his wallet and waved it in my face!"

Karen wrenched free of Richard's hold and faced the woman. Her eyes flared with rage. "You're lying!" she hissed, her control breaking.

"Karen!" Richard eyed the reporter anxiously. "Let's drop it," he said, grabbing her and pushing her toward the door.

"Let me go, Richard!" Karen cried furiously. "She's lying!" She twisted out of his grip and approached the girl.

"Lying? Why would I lie? Your fine, respectable husband tried to rape me. *He's* the one who's lying!" Pam screamed, leaning toward Karen, her face flushed with anger. "You married a real sick man, lady, do you know that? Sick! Perverted!" Her horrible words echoed throughout the police station.

All at once, Karen lunged for the girl. Suddenly the photographer started snapping pictures, as Sid and Richard tried to get Karen under control.

"All right, that's enough!" Spatz yelled. "Break it up, all of you. Sid, Richard, get out of here!"

The two men finally managed to push Karen out of the office as Pam continued

screaming angry accusations. The newspaperman was taking down every word.

"That was some performance," Spatz said
as the teenager finally quieted herself. He
turned to Carney. "Did you get it all?" he
demanded sarcastically.

"Yeah," Carney said, not looking up from
his notepad.

"You know, Carney, you're a real—"

"Saint," the journalist supplied sweetly,
and lifted his pencil from the pad. He looked
at the lieutenant. "That's what my mother
used to call me. Saint." He smiled.

Spatz shook his head. "Sid Fairgate's
innocent and you know it. Why even run the
story?"

Carney shrugged. "It's news. It'll sell
papers. Besides, how do you know he's
innocent?"

The lieutenant shook his head and glanced
over at Pam Messinger. She sat quietly
now, her face red, eyes puffy. Her hands
gripped the edge of the desk top. Then
she looked up, almost as if she sensed
someone was watching her. When her eyes
met the lieutenant's, they narrowed in a
nasty glare.

What evil lay behind those young eyes?
Spatz wondered. Did she really intend to
destroy Sid Fairgate?

Karen was scrambling eggs for breakfast. Her
hands were going through the motions, but
her eyes stared blankly out the kitchen

window. None of her attention was focused on her breakfast preparations. This was a morning like no other.

Turning off the heat under the eggs, she removed the cover from another saucepan and gave the hashbrowns a stir. Cooking oil shot out from the pan, spattering her arm with hot liquid.

She backed away from the pan, the burns shocking her back to reality. *Poor Sid.* That had been all she could think through most of the sleepless night. He had to stumble into something like this. Sometimes he was too good, *too* kind to his fellow creatures. Why couldn't he be more cautious, a little less trusting?

Any thoughts that Sid might actually have tried to rape the girl had quickly been dispelled by the utter absurdity of the charge. Karen knew that she didn't have to worry about it, and she hoped the rest of Knots Landing would agree with her.

By the kitchen counter, Diana was talking on the phone. She was wrapped in a bathrobe, her hair in curlers.

"What do you mean, *would* I? Of course I would! That would be incredible!" she cried happily. "Sure, I'll rehearse as much as you want—all day, all night, every day of the week!"

"Right," Eric mumbled from the kitchen table where he pushed his eggs around on his plate. The fourteen-year-old turned to his brother Michael, two years his junior, who sat unhappily before his untouched breakfast.

"Sure, I'm ready. Come right over!" Diana said, then remembered her curlers and bathrobe. "Well, make that fifteen minutes, okay? See you outside. 'Bye!" She slammed the phone down. "That was Kevin," she began, turning excitedly to her mother and brothers.

"No kidding," Eric said, sneering at her.

She ignored him. "He said they want to add a girl singer to Zarris. Guess who they want?"

"Your best friend Linda?" Eric asked dryly.

"She sings better than you," Mike said, and stuffed a forkful of eggs into his mouth.

"Boys," Karen said sternly, and turned down the heat on the potatoes. Where was Sid? He'd been upstairs so long.

"Very funny, brats," Diana said, sticking her tongue out. "They want *me* to sing with Zarris? Isn't that fabulous?"

"That's wonderful, honey," Karen said, with a tentative smile.

"So it's your voice Kevin likes about you?" Eric asked.

Diana turned to her brother. "That . . . and other things." She turned and ran for the door, almost knocking over her father as he entered the kitchen. "Daddy, I—"

"I know, I overheard," he said, smiling.

Karen turned to Sid. He looked tired.

"Do you need a ride?" he asked Diana.

"No. Kevin's stopping by."

"Good. Just—just don't ever hitchhike, okay, Diana?" Sid said, looking at her closely.

She smiled. "I'm not *that* crazy, Daddy."

"Good." Sid touched her shoulder and she was gone, racing up to her bedroom.

"Hello," Karen said, switching off the potatoes. Perfectly timed, she decided, peeking under the saucepan lid. She carried the pan to the table and piled the potatoes onto Sid's plate. "How was San Luis Obispo?" Karen asked, when she could think of nothing else to say. "How was Abby? I forgot to ask last night with all the excitement."

Sid smiled. "She had everything done. Everything! The house was virtually closed up by the time I got there. But she kept on asking me to stay just in case something happened." Sid shook his head wearily.

"Did it?" Karen asked.

"No."

Eric and Michael rose from the table and made their escape from the kitchen.

"So she wasn't so broken up about her divorce that she couldn't pack?" Karen asked wryly.

"She didn't seem upset; in fact, she looked like some weight had been lifted off her. I haven't seen her smile so much in a long time."

Karen nodded. "Figures. *I* thought Jeff was a great guy, and that he and Abby were good together. I guess we just don't think alike."

"Abby's leaving today for San Diego. I told

her if she wanted to take a break from all the driving she could stop by here."

Karen's face hardened as she cleaned the last of the egg from the pan. "Did she say she would?" she wondered, scraping the pan harder than necessary,

"You know my little sis," Sid said. "She makes decisions on the spot." He took a bite of the eggs.

"I called Richard this morning," Karen said. "Woke him up. He said he's going to see that girl."

"Sounds like a good idea."

"Maybe not. I think we should let Irv do this. Criminal law isn't Richard's speciality."

"It isn't Irv's either," Sid pointed out. "He does our taxes and business stuff. I'm sure Richard will be fine." He watched Karen take two biscuits from the oven and place them on a plate with butter and jam. "He should see the girl, try to talk some sense into her. I thought about doing that myself."

"Doing what?" Karen asked, alarmed.

"Seeing the girl."

"Sid!" Karen sank down into a chair opposite him. "Can't you understand? That girl's nothing but trouble for you. Don't see her, don't call her, don't get within ten feet of her. She's poison, Sid. She could scream rape again. What would you do then?"

Sid cradled his coffee mug in his hands. His eyes narrowed. "I never thought about that."

Karen rose and walked over to him.

"Richard can see the girl. Okay? But you've got to remember one thing, honey. She doesn't play fair. She's *not* a good person." Karen kissed his forehead. "I know you like to see the best in people, but in this case . . . she just doesn't deserve your sympathy, Sid."

Sid pushed his plate aside. "I know," he agreed with a sigh. "I *can't* feel sorry for her. After all, look what she's trying to do to me."

Karen was surprised at the bitterness in his voice.

Cool, salty Pacific breezes blew in over Seaview Circle as a blue Volvo station wagon turned into the cul-de-sac. It passed Kenny and Ginger Ward's house, then the Averys' home and finally parked at the curb in front of Sid and Karen Fairgate's house.

Abby Cunningham, fresh from her divorce, looked like she was ready to take on the world. Her vibrant blond hair framed an incredibly beautiful face, with piercing eyes and sensual lips.

Behind her in the car sat her two children, Olivia, a pretty, delicate nine-year-old, and Brian, at seven a curly-haired bundle of energy.

"Come on, quiet down, kids. Okay?" Her voice revealed her irritation. Several hours with her children in the car had frayed her nerves.

"That's Uncle Sid's house!" Olivia shouted.

"Olivia!" Abby stopped the car, then turned and glared at her daughter. "I've had a hard drive!" she complained. "Keep it down, okay?"

"Keep it down, okay?" the little girl said, imitating her mother perfectly.

"Not again!" Abby said. "I thought I cured you of that!"

"Not again! I thought I cured you of that!"

"Oh, brother," Brian said.

"Oh, brother."

The boy produced his yellow plastic trumpet and tooted on it.

Abby sighed. She was beginning to realize that being a single mother was twice as hard as being a married one.

Karen and Sid Fairgate appeared at their door to greet her. Steeling herself, Abby smiled into the rearview mirror, slung her purse over her shoulder, and got out of the car. Olivia and Brian followed after her.

"Abby, welcome!" Karen said with a bright smile.

"Hi," Abby returned. They hugged briefly, then Abby stepped back. "Hello, Sid."

"Hello, Abby," Sid said and embraced her.

Eric and Michael trailed out of the house to greet the guests—with little enthusiasm.

"Hello, Olivia," Eric said.

"Hello, Olivia," the girl repeated.

"What?" Eric asked.

"What?"

"This is a new game," Abby started to explain.

"This is a new game."

"She started playing it on the way here."

"She started playing it on the way here." Olivia's face was expressionless as she mimicked her mother.

"Cute," Karen said.

"Cute."

"How'd you like the trip down here, Brian?" Michael asked. "Must've been real fun with a parrot for a sister."

The boy tooted his horn as the group headed for the house.

Abby slung an arm around Sid's shoulder. "You got home all right last night, I see," she said, smiling.

"Well, as a matter of fact—" Sid began.

"What happened?" Abby asked.

"What happened?" Olivia repeated.

"It's a long story," Karen said, and held her hand over Olivia's mouth. "Inside," she told the girl, who politely obeyed.

"Welcome to Knots Landing, sis," Sid said, his face frozen in a worried smile. "Welcome to our peaceful little town."

Karen was trying to concentrate on Abby's monologue, but she felt uneasy. Around her living room sat her husband, the Averys, Gary and Val Ewing, and Ginger Ward. Karen had thrown together an impromptu gathering.

Calm down, she told herself firmly. *Stop worrying about Sid. If Walter Spatz says not to worry, don't worry!*

By the time she cleared her thoughts of Sid's trial she realized that Richard Avery was staring at Abby, and had been ever since he'd joined the party. A quick glance at Laura told Karen that his wife hadn't even noticed. Karen forced a smile and joined in the conversation. She certainly had enough on her mind not to be wondering about Richard's fascination with Abby!

"I'm taking the kids to San Diego, and Jeff'll move to the Los Angeles area," Abby was saying. "I don't want Olivia and Brian very far away from their father. But I don't want Jeff too near, either."

"San Diego?" Laura asked. "Why there?"

"I've visited it in the past. Jeff and I took the kids to the zoo and Sea World on one trip, remember? I like it, I guess." She smiled. "Anyway, it's full of sailors . . . so I can never get *too* lonely there."

Sid chuckled, but his smile was forced. Abby spotted it instantly.

"Oh, Sid, I didn't mean to embarrass you," she said sweetly.

"You didn't embarrass me," he said, still smiling.

"You offended his morals," Richard muttered dryly.

She smirked. "Sid just can't stand the fact that I've grown up."

"You haven't grown up," Sid said, smiling genuinely now. "I'm fourteen years older than Abby," he said to Richard. "All these years later that's still true. She'll never catch up with me." He winked at his sister.

"We'll see about that," Abby said.

"Don't listen to the guy. He's still an old-fashioned moralist at heart," Richard said.

Abby clutched her coffee cup. "I *don't* listen to him."

Karen turned to Laura. "So, how's the new job?"

"Fine," she began. "When I started it was just a job—nothing more. But now, real estate's—"

"Real estate's bit her on the neck," Richard volunteered, joining in on the conversation. "She's become one of them, been initiated into their club. She wakes at dusk to rise and prowl for fresh houses," Richard said sarcastically. "Laura, you're not in the business. You're licking stamps and typing letters. That doesn't count as real estate work."

Laura grimaced. "I had to type some names on form letters and address a hundred envelopes today," she explained, her cheeks pink with embarrassment.

"And made coffee," Richard added.

"Right." Laura's voice grew soft.

"Life's tough in the real estate game," her husband mused.

"Richard, shut up!" Karen told him good-naturedly.

Brian ran into the room, tooting his plastic horn.

"My son," Abby said, rolling her eyes.

The seven-year-old started to race around

the room, accompanying himself on his horn. Abby put down her plate of cake and scooped him up into her arms. She gave him a big kiss, then set him on the floor.

"He's got a terrific vocabulary!" Karen laughed. "Does he always talk this much? I don't think I've heard him say a word since you got here."

Abby frowned. "Brian's stubborn."

"Where's your sister, Brian?" Val asked, bending down to speak to the boy. "I haven't met her yet."

Brian tooted.

"Upstairs," Abby translated.

Val flashed a grin. "Abby Cunningham, don't you think I can hear for myself?"

"Maybe you should leave her alone for a while," Abby suggested as Val started toward the stairs. "She's still getting settled."

Val smiled. "Well, then I'll meet her later on."

Brian dashed to the coffee table, stuffed a cookie in his mouth, and then tore out of the room.

Just then, there came a knock at the front door. Karen rose to answer it and Kenny Ward appeared, smiling.

"Kenny." Karen frowned. "I didn't expect to see you here. What do you want?"

"Ginger. Is she here?" the handsome young record producer asked. He looked over Karen's shoulder.

Ginger's eyes met his.

Richard came to the door and stood behind

Karen. "Yes, Ginger's here," he said. "And I don't think she wants to see you."

"Please, Richard," Ginger said, moving to the door. "That's enough."

Across the living room, Abby turned. She caught sight of Kenny and smiled in appreciation. She let her eyes move over him, then approached him, obviously enjoying the view. "Who's this?" she asked Ginger.

"Her husband," Kenny said quickly.

"We're separated, remember, Kenny?" Ginger turned to Abby. "Abby Cunningham, Kenny Ward. Abby is Sid's sister from San Luis Obispo."

They shook hands. Abby let him keep her hand in his for a moment, while Kenny gazed at her.

"You're cute," Abby said, flashing him a smile.

"Thanks." He laughed.

"I think you and Ginger have some talking to do. I'll see you later, Kenny. Won't I?"

"Sure." He smiled.

Ginger moved away from the rest of the guests, and signalled for Kenny to follow her. He obeyed, but his eyes lingered on Abby as she returned to the living room.

"So, how've you been?" he asked Ginger, returning his gaze to her.

"Just fine," she said shortly. She kept her eyes averted.

"Really?" Kenny frowned. "You're not just saying that, are you?"

She looked up at him. "Why did you come here, Kenny?"

"Just wanted to say hello, maybe talk to you. You weren't at home, but I figured there was a party over here, so I took a chance."

"There's nothing left to talk about," Ginger said, shaking her head. "We're separated, and that's the way I want it to stay. Can't you understand?"

"No."

"That's what a separation is, Kenny. It means separate. We have nothing to talk about."

Kenny sighed loudly. "But we're still married, Ginger. Did you forget *that*?"

"Apparently you did, or else you wouldn't be living with that singer friend of yours, Sylvie."

"I'm staying with her. I didn't have anywhere else to go after you threw me out," he said irritably.

Ginger shook her head. "You are incredible, do you know that? I walked in on the two of you. I saw what you were doing. It's not like I don't know how you've been acting, how sacred you held our marriage vows."

"Look, Ginger, I don't want to argue—"

"Then you shouldn't have come here," she said icily.

"Can't we even—"

"No!" Ginger said harshly. "Go back to your mistress."

Sid walked in to find Ginger and Kenny

glaring at each other.

"Kenny!" Sid said. "When did you get here?"

Kenny forced a smile. "Hi, Sid."

"Come on in. Have some coffee." Sid slapped Kenny's back and pulled him toward the coffee table.

Ginger watched the two men join the other guests. She was furious—at Kenny for coming here, and now at Sid for asking him to stay!

On the couch, Abby had cornered Gary Ewing, ignoring Richard Avery's leering looks and intense interest. "I've heard so much about you, how you're J. R. Ewing's brother and everything." Abby gazed at him.

"Good things?" Gary asked pleasantly.

"Of course." She lowered her eyes. "But then, we expect nothing but the best from a Ewing." A knowing smile touched her lips. "I've always heard that Texas boys do *everything* better."

Gary smiled but did not have a chance to reply. At that moment, Olivia stomped down the stairs. "Mom!" she yelled above the general chatter.

"What is it, honey?" Abby asked, reluctantly turning away from the striking blond man.

"Where's my book?" her daughter asked, pouting.

"It's packed. Get one of Diana's, okay?"

"Okay." Olivia walked forlornly back upstairs.

Val's maternal instincts couldn't be ignored. She set her plate down and followed the sad little girl out of the room.

"Well, Abby," Richard said as the woman turned back to Gary. "I know you've fallen in love with all of us men. But what do you think of Knots Landing?"

"It's nice," she said, uncertainly.

"Life in the fast lane, baby," Richard murmured, moving closer to her on the couch.

She turned to him with a condescending smile. "I can imagine what you drive." She stood and walked away as Gary laughed.

Olivia sat on the frilly bed and stared at the stuffed dolls that festooned Diana's bedroom. She held a book in her lap, unopened. She sighed miserably.

Poor child, Val thought as she peered around the corner of the opened door. *Might as well try to make her feel good. Abby's having such a good time—no sense in bothering her.* She knocked gently on the door. Olivia looked up as Val walked into the room.

"Hello, Olivia," she said sweetly.

"Hello, Olivia."

Val raised a questioning eyebrow, then remembered the child's game. "I'm Val."

"I'm Val." She stared at the wall.

The Southern woman shook her head. "What a coincidence! I don't meet many other Vals."

"What a coincidence," Olivia said. "I

don't meet many other Vals."

"I hear an echo," she said, laughing.

"I hear an echo."

Val frowned, trying to understand the little girl's troubles. Olivia looked up at her from the bed, obviously unhappy and bored.

"Well," Val said.

"Well."

The woman suddenly hurried toward the bed and spoke quickly. "You know, Olivia, I really wish you wouldn't—"

"You know, Olivia, I really wish you wouldn't—" the child began.

"—repeat everything I say because even though I've just met you, I like you and you remind me of my daughter—she's older, of course, but you still remind me of her and I'd really like to be your friend!"

"—repeat everything I said . . . I mean I say . . . because . . . because . . ." Olivia stopped, defeated. She frowned and looked down at the book, then opened it and pretended to read.

Val sat on the edge of the bed. "Did I win?" she asked quietly.

Olivia shook her head.

Val was surprised. "I didn't? Well, did you just stop playing?"

She smiled. "Yes."

"I don't blame you, Olivia. It isn't very easy." She watched as the girl went through the motions of reading. "Can't we just talk, Olivia? I'd like to be friends with you."

Olivia looked hesitantly at Val, saw Val's

smile, and lowered the book to her lap.

"Something bothering you?" Val asked softly, not wanting to prod her too far.

Olivia shook her head, then nodded. "We're—they're—" She sighed. "Daddy and Mommy are getting a divorce."

Val bit her lip.

"I don't know why," the little girl cried, despair filling her eyes. "Everything was nice."

"Olivia," Val soothed.

"I hate divorce!" The girl pouted.

Val touched Olivia's arm tenderly. "That's not an easy game to play, either. Is it?"

"No," Olivia said. "No one wins." She looked back at her book.

Chapter Three
Dangerous Underestimate

"I'm sorry to imply that I don't have complete faith in you, Richard," Karen said as she stood talking with the lawyer and her husband later on during the party. "I'm just so worried about this whole terrible mess."

"It's all right," he said with a curt smile. "But lose that worried look, Karen. Sid's in no danger. Everything'll be fine." He turned to Sid. "You trust me, don't you?"

"I certainly do." He flashed a grin.

"Yeah, well, that's just the kind of guy you are. You'd leave your car unlocked with the keys in the ignition, down on Wharf Street after two in the morning, and expect to see it an hour later."

"I'm not that bad," Sid insisted.

"You're not the challenge, Sid. It's Karen." He turned to her. "She's the one I have to convince. I can handle this case."

"Look, Richard," Karen said patiently.

"I'm allowed some worry here, don't you think? This isn't a game. This is real, and it's happening to my husband." She looked at Sid, then back to Richard. "Don't take this personally, but I don't want anything to go wrong."

"I don't take it personally, and nothing will go wrong." Richard scratched his chin. "But go ahead. Call another lawyer if it'll ease your mind. He'll just tell you the same thing I've been saying—that Sid's not in any real trouble."

"You wouldn't mind?" Karen asked quickly.

"No."

Gary Ewing joined the trio from the other side of the living room. "Look, Karen, I hate to barge in on this, but I have to agree with Richard. Call a criminal lawyer if it'll make you feel better. There's no real reason not to."

The woman turned to Richard. "Don't take it personally if I do."

"No chance." Richard Avery stuffed one hand into his pocket and looked at her, smirking.

Sid left the group to stand beside Abby, who rose from the couch. "Abby, I haven't really visited with you since you arrived."

"A lot has been happening," his sister informed him, glancing at Kenny, who stood nearby. She smiled dreamily.

Sid nodded, not catching her meaning. "Sure has. Don't remind me!"

"Do you have any scotch, Karen?" Richard

asked, looking over at the bar. "I've had about as much coffee as I can stand."

Karen hesitated for a moment. "Of course, Richard. Please, help yourself."

When Richard went off to the bar, Gary grabbed hold of Karen's arm.

"Look," he said. "Thanks for your concern, but don't ruin the party on my account."

Karen scowled at him. "I have no idea what you're talking about, Gary Ewing!"

"Come on. This party. Coffee and cake?" He smiled. "I can be around other people drinking. Just because I'm a recovering alcoholic doesn't mean you have to lock up the liquor. I can resist booze."

Karen mussed his blond hair. "I never thought about it," she said seriously.

Gary looked at her intently. "Come on."

She felt her face grow warm. "Maybe I did," Karen admitted gently, and winked.

Olivia lay on Diana's bed, staring up at the ceiling, while Val sat patiently reading a children's book to her. Her soft voice filled the small room, rhythmic and comforting.

" 'Patches ran down the alley, dodging the rain puddles that blinded her eyes, the trash that made her feet slip and slide, and the dark, mysterious shadows that other dogs might hide in.' "

Val looked down at Olivia. The girl seemed to be enjoying the story, though it was a bit young for her age. " 'The dog's barks echoed down the alley—and then grew louder. Patches couldn't look over her shoulder because she was afraid of what she'd see— now she heard the barks of three, then four dogs. She raced as fast as she could on her four feet.' "

Olivia stirred and settled herself in Val's outstretched arm. She cuddled the child. "Want me to read some more of the story, Olivia?" she murmured.

"Please!" The girl sounded eager.

Val smiled and went on with her story.

From the doorway, Abby watched Val reading to her daughter with a peculiar mixture of admiration and contempt. That woman seemed to have a special way with children. She was even better with Abby's children than Abby herself. Val had cured Olivia of her annoying habit of repeating everything. Even Brian was calmer when Val was around.

Abby slipped away from the door. As she started down the hall she felt a twinge of guilt. Was *she* a good mother? If she was, shouldn't she be up in the bedroom reading to her daughter?

Abby sighed. Olivia wouldn't sit still if she tried to read to her. It was clear that Val possessed a magic that Abby lacked. Abby's eyes narrowed. Well, she had better things to do. Bracing herself, Abby descended the stairs to rejoin the party.

* * *

Pam Messinger pulled a can of cheap beer from the refrigerator and slammed the door shut. A cigarette with an inch of ash dangled from her lips. As she turned, the ash scattered all over her white T-shirt.

"You shouldn't smoke," a large, attractive woman with flaming red hair told her. She was sitting in front of a television set, but her mind was clearly not on the game show.

"I know, Mom," Pam said mechanically. She looked around the filthy, junk-strewn apartment and sighed. "This place is a pit," she said, glancing at the stained blue couch, a wobbly dinette table, assorted t.v. trays and a moth-eaten recliner. Wastebaskets were overflowing, and trash littered the tiny apartment.

"Well, you shouldn't smoke," Selma Messinger said.

"Yeah, and you shouldn't drink. Big deal." She flicked the rest of the cigarette ash on the floor.

"Hey!" Selma snapped. "I spent a lot of time cleaning that floor."

Pam sneered. "Yeah? When? Last year?" She tipped the beer can up, draining it.

"Pam, there's no need to guzzle—"

Pam threw the can against the television, a small black and white model that had been obsolete for years. Amber waves of beer spread over the silent image of a game show host. The set hadn't had sound for over a year.

"Don't you respect anything?" Selma

demanded wearily. "I know you don't respect me, or yourself. But I don't deserve your contempt. I wasn't always down in the dumps, you know," she said haughtily.

Pam rolled her eyes and dragged heavily on the cigarette. "Here it comes again."

"You shut your mouth, young lady!" Selma said. "I used to be high society, you know. I went to all the parties, the premieres, the best stores. I was rich, then I lost it. You know how?"

"Spent it on men," Pam said dully.

Selma glared at her daughter. "He stole it from me. That man *stole* it from me!"

"Mom, you inherited $750,000 from Daddy when he died. What did you do with it?" she asked, disinterestedly.

"How the hell am I supposed to remember something like that? It was fifteen years ago."

Pam shook her head and crushed out the cigarette on one of the t.v. trays. "You're something, you know that, Mother?"

"I *was*," she said. "I may be down now, but I was something, and don't you ever forget it!" She punctuated the last phrase with her finger. Then she picked up an old magazine that lay under her chair, and opened it to the word search page. She ran a pencil down a column of letters. By moving it horizontally, vertically, and diagonally, Selma Messinger might eventually find all thirty gardening terms hidden in the seven inch square of letters, if her daughter left her alone. It might take her all evening. But what *else* was there to do, anyhow? she wondered dully.

"So, what do you think?" Karen asked Ginger as they stood in the kitchen. Karen's party was still going full blast in the living room, but she was feeling worn out.

"Oh, Karen, I don't know," Ginger said. "I'm afraid I'm no good at things like this. I don't know anything about trials and court cases."

"I know, but I just wanted your opinion. I mean, Richard says I should go ahead and call another lawyer for a second opinion, but—"

"Then I guess he knows what he's talking about, right?" The gentle woman smiled. "It certainly couldn't do any harm to call someone else, could it?"

Karen shrugged. "I suppose not. You're right, Ginger. Thanks." She smiled. "I'll call Irv tomorrow. I know it's Sunday, but I'll just call him at home. I know I shouldn't worry, but I really feel as if Sid's life is in this girl's hands . . . and I don't trust her . . .

Early Sunday morning, Eric handed the newspaper to Brian, who, still half-asleep and dressed in his pajamas, had followed his cousins out into the garage.

"Give this to my parents," Eric said, his face red. He grabbed his bike and rode off with Michael, who hadn't said a word all morning.

Brian tooted on his horn and carried the

paper back inside the house.

"Toot-toot-toot!" Brian trumpeted as he marched into Sid and Karen's bedroom.

Karen shook herself awake, and sat up in bed. "Brian! Stop that, please!"

The boy dropped the paper on the bed, then turned and scurried out the door.

"What is it?" Sid asked groggily, rubbing his face and yawning.

"Just Brian with the paper," she answered and lazily flipped it open, scanning the headlines. The stock market had dropped again, there was yet another hotel employees strike, and a typhoon had hit a small Pacific island. Skimming over the local news, Karen suddenly gasped.

"Something wrong?" Sid mumbled sleepily.

"Sid, wake up. Look at this!" Karen spread the paper flat out on the blanket.

Sid pulled himself up straight and glanced at the paper. "Oh, no . . ." His eyes widened in horror.

There in bold black and white was a graphic, ugly picture. Sid Fairgate, looking mad and disheveled, stood in the foreground, one hand reaching for his wife. Karen was making a grab for an unfocused figure—presumably Pam Messinger's—while Richard stood by looking helpless.

"I don't believe it," Sid said. "That reporter and that photographer!"

Above the picture was the terrible headline: LOCAL CAR DEALER HIT WITH

SCANDALOUS CHARGE.

Karen stared at the curtains, behind which shone the hot California sun. A flurry of emotions passed across her face. Then suddenly she slammed her fist at the picture.

"Now, Karen—"

"Richard promised us this wouldn't happen! It's already begun! You're being tried and hanged by the papers and there hasn't even been a preliminary hearing yet!"

Sid was silent, staring at the picture.

Karen's eyes searched her husband's face. "Sid, what are we going to do?" she asked desperately.

He looked up from the picture and reached out for Karen's hand. "Fight," he said in a low, ominous voice.

Sid rose from the kitchen table. "Thanks for the lunch, Karen. Think I'll go tinker on the car."

"Okay." She waited until he was out of the room, then put down the dishes she was washing, and picked up the phone. She quickly dialed a number.

The phone rang twice at the other end.

"Hello, Irv?"

"That's right," a pleasant male voice said.

"Karen Fairgate. I'm sorry to call you at home, but—"

"Karen Fairgate? How are you? How's old Sid?" Irv asked with genuine concern.

"That's why I'm calling," Karen said. "We need some legal advice."

"That's why I'm here. What can I do for you? Business problems?"

"No, nothing like that, unfortunately. We need help with a criminal case."

The line was silent for a moment.

"Irv?"

"Yeah, Karen, I'm right here. What's going on over there?"

Karen frowned. "I don't know any other way to say this, so I'll just plunge right in. Sid's been accused of attempting to rape a teen-age girl."

Irv guffawed. "Come on, Karen!"

"This is serious, Irv! I wish I was kidding, believe me. Fortunately, Walter Spatz was there and released Sid on his own recognizance. The preliminary hearing's Tuesday. I wasn't so worried about this whole mess until I saw the morning paper. Have you read it?"

"No, never before breakfast."

"Read it, Irv. Sid was charged with assault and assault with attempt to rape, among other things. We thought it might be settled quickly, get thrown out of court, or something. We didn't expect a media circus. The morning news ran a short report on it on the radio." Karen sighed. "It must be all over town by now."

"So you're looking for a good criminal lawyer?"

"Right. One who can pull Sid out of this whole mess."

"What happened?" Irv asked.

"He picked up a teen-age girl who was in trouble with a couple of men on the street. Now she's accusing him of trying to rape her."

"I see." Irv was silent for a moment. "Stan Loesser," he said. "Best man for the job. He's competent, experienced, and wins most of his cases. His home phone's 555-6938. Tell him I referred you."

Karen scribbled the number down. "Okay. Thanks a lot, Irv."

"Don't panic, Karen," he said.

"I'm not panicking, I'm going out of my mind. But I'll do everything I can to see that Sid's cleared of this. I don't want to leave anything to chance."

"Of course. Perfectly understandable. Say hello to Sid for me, and tell him he has all my support."

"Thanks, Irv," Karen said, and hung up. She stared at the number on her pad, then quickly dialed the lawyer.

Dressed in overalls, Sid bent over his car's engine and frowned. The familiar working parts seemed alien to him, his mind was so clouded with frustration, anger and fear. The garage felt smaller somehow, and Sid had to fight off feelings of claustrophobia.

He banged his fist against the raised hood, unable to control his conflicting emotions.

"Hello in there," a soft voice called. Abby stepped into the light of the bare over-hanging bulb.

57

"Hi, Abby," Sid said, managing a smile.

"I thought I might find you here."

"Karen's in the house," he said, turning away and wiping his hands on his coveralls.

"No luck with the car today?" Abby asked sympathetically.

"No." He moved to face her. "I can't seem to think about anything but the case."

Abby reached out to touch his shoulder. "I know. Sid, I can't believe this is happening to you." Her eyes spoke of her compassion for her brother.

"Neither can I." Sid's voice broke slightly. "But I'm trying."

"Do you think this girl will stick to her story?"

Her brother laughed. "I don't know what she'll do. You know, Abby, it's all my fault."

"No, it isn't, Sid! Just because you picked up that girl doesn't mean you knew she'd—"

"That's not what I meant. I called her bluff, Abby. When I didn't give her the hundred dollars, she said she'd scream rape. I told her she might as well do it since there was a police car across the street." He swallowed loudly. "I never thought she'd do it," he admitted.

"Don't blame yourself, Sid!" Abby insisted. "That doesn't accomplish anything."

"No, but it gives me something to do."

Abby's eyes turned icy. "Why don't you think of ways to get back at her?"

Sid chuckled. "Not my style. But I can't

think of any way to prove my innocence. In the long run it comes down to her word against mine."

"Exactly! And her word is worthless." She put an arm around her brother's shoulder. "I know we haven't always seen eye to eye on everything, Sid, but you know I'm behind you in this, don't you?"

He smiled. "Yes. Thanks for your support."

"I really don't think you have anything to worry about, Sid. No one believes what's written in the papers."

"I hope not."

She smiled. "If you can't relax, at least don't be so hard on yourself."

"I'm not the only one affected by this, you know. Karen, the kids, the whole neighborhood's going to go through this with me."

Abby shrugged. "You'll come out clean in the end, Sid. I know it." She smiled and kissed him impulsively on the cheek. "I just have this feeling everything will work out all right."

"Hey, Joey! Don't let your sister go over to Seaview Circle," a skinny young boy said to his friend as they stood playing volleyball on Knots Landing Beach.

"Why not, Ron?" Joey asked.

"Because Michael Fairgate's father lives there." He wiggled his eyebrows suggestively.

"Shut up, Ron!" Michael yelled, ignoring

the volleyball as it went by him.

"We all know what Michael Fairgate's dad does at night," Ron said, leering at the boy. "We read it in the paper. He likes—"

Michael's face was red, his heart pounding.

"Shut up! Shut your mouth! You're lying!" he cried, and pushed the boy backward.

"You wanna prove it?" Ron demanded—and punched Michael's jaw.

Pain shot through the boy, blinding him temporarily. Michael jabbed out wildly at Ron, and missed.

Large, powerful hands gripped Michael's wrists and pulled him away from the fight.

"Leave me alone!" Michael yelled.

"What's going on here?" the older man asked.

Another adult grabbed Ron, who was kicking and screaming, and tried to calm him down.

"Ask Ron!" Michael said. "Ask *him* what's going on here." Michael stared at the ground.

"You know already," Ron said. "Didn't you read the papers?" A few boys laughed.

Michael struggled free from the grown-up's hands and ran toward the parking lot. His bare feet dug into the sand as he hurried away from the game, his face burning.

"Aren't you going to finish the game?" a voice called.

Michael ran until he reached his bicycle, which stood in the parking lot.

On the beach, Ron shook himself free from

the man who had held him back. His eyes followed after Michael as the young boy disappeared. "Mike Fairgate's father raped a teen-age girl," he said, his voice filled with contempt.

Someone snickered. "Yeah. No girl's safe at night with Fairgate on the loose."

Karen drove the short distance to Stan Loesser's house, her mind in a whirl. Next to her on the seat lay the newspaper article, the picture muted in the intense sunlight.

By the time she pulled up before the two-story house nestled high above the ocean, Karen had calmed herself. She walked up to the front door and pushed the button confidently.

A handsome man in his mid-forties appeared after a moment. He smiled at her. "Karen Fairgate?"

"Yes, hello, Mr. Loesser." She smiled at him, clutching the article.

"Please, come in, Mrs. Fairgate." He stepped back. "You look familiar. Didn't we meet at a party a few months back?" the black-haired man asked, eyeing her curiously.

"It's possible, but I'm afraid I don't remember."

Stan showed her to the living room. Karen sat on the couch and slapped the article down on the coffee table as Stan seated himself opposite her. "Is this bad?" Karen asked. "I mean, as bad as it looks? I know it's just the newspaper, but they can be pretty powerful."

Stan read it over and grimaced. "It's just a story," he said slowly.

Karen looked at him. "Really?" She didn't sound convinced.

Loesser sighed. "Okay, Mrs. Fairgate. The story itself isn't so bad, but what the girl says about her character and past could be trouble." He looked at the article again, searching the columns. "Listen to this, for instance: 'I'm not a good girl. I've been around—had more boyfriends than I could count. I don't always go home to my mother every night, get it?' She doesn't try to hide her past, that's for sure."

"Let me see that a minute," Karen said and took the article. She scanned the print. " 'It's my life, and I can live it any way I like. But that doesn't give anyone the right to rape me. Sid Fairgate committed a crime when he tried to force me to sleep with him. I don't care if his lawyer brings my last ten lovers to court. It doesn't make what he did to me right.' "

"That's an effective slant," Loesser said, watching the woman beside him intently.

"Very effective." Karen nodded. "Because it's the truth. She has every right to lead whatever kind of life she wants, but no one has the right to rape her. But I'm just afraid that . . . well . . ."

"That she'll get sympathy because she's being honest?" Stan finished for her. "Are you thinking that the jury will believe her, even though they might not like her?"

Karen looked startled. "The jury? Mr. Loesser, you don't think it's going to come to that, do you?"

"Probably not," Stan said, shaking his head. "And please, call me Stan, okay, Karen?"

"Okay."

"Karen, I'm sure Richard Avery will do as good a job for Sid as I could."

"Really?"

"Well, I don't have the paperwork here— the girl's statement, arrest reports. But if it's a simple case of Pam Messinger's word against Sid's, the only defense is to contrast the characters of the two parties involved."

Karen nodded. "That's Richard's plan."

"Avery works for Pincus, Simpson and Lyle, doesn't he?"

"That's right."

"I'm sure he'll have the firm behind him if he gets in over his head. That should ease your mind, Karen."

"But this is a criminal case, and they aren't a criminal law firm," Karen said anxiously.

"But Larry Hanover's associated with them. Hanover was one of the best lawyers in the area for years, a fantastic criminal attorney. Even old man Simpson was a prosecutor, years ago." He studied her across the table. "So stop worrying, okay?"

She managed a brave smile. "I'll try."

"At least you'll have nothing to worry about in Richard Avery's presentation of your case," he said soothingly.

Karen looked at him bleakly. "That's not very reassuring, Stan. Do you mean there's something I *should* be worrying about?"

Loesser shrugged. "It's hard to say. Criminal cases like this—especially those involving rape—can go in some pretty unpredictible directions." He eyed her thoughtfully. "No matter how good your lawyer is, you can never prepare for all the surprises in store."

His words sent a chill down her spine.

Eric Fairgate sat on the front steps of his house, staring morosely out at the deserted road.

All day, wherever he'd gone—to the beach, the store, even to friends' houses—people had sneered at him and cast him leering looks that weren't hard to decipher. Apparently all of Knots Landing had read the cursed newspaper article, and they treated him like dirt.

Michael rode up on his bike, jumped off it, and let it fall in the front yard. His chin was bloodied.

"Hey, Michael!" Eric called. "Are you all right?"

The boy glanced at him, cheeks puffy, eyes red, clothing torn. "What's it look like to you?" he asked savagely, then ran through the door into the kitchen.

"Hey, Michael!" Sid said as his son shot past him in the kitchen. "What—"

"It's just a little cut," Michael said, slowing on his way to the stairs. "I fell on my bike going over a hole." He ran out of the room.

Sid turned and saw Eric walk into the room.

"It's okay, Dad," he said. "The boys must've roughed him up on the beach."

"Roughed him up?" Sid asked, astonished. "Since when is that okay?"

"We know it's not true," Eric said weakly. "What the paper said, I mean."

Sid looked at his son. "What about Michael?" he asked. "What does he think?"

Eric looked unhappy. "The same thing, Dad. We both believe you . . ."

Sid waited. When the boy fell silent, Sid lay a hand on his shoulder. "But something's still bothering you, isn't it, son?"

Eric shied away from his father's touch. "It doesn't matter," he said, and turned toward the living room.

"Son, I'm talking to you. I asked you to tell me what's wrong."

"It's just that . . . well, why didn't you just leave her on the street?"

"What?"

"Why'd you ever let that girl into your car in the first place? This *never* would have happened if you hadn't picked her up!" Eric stepped back, his face burning red with shame and anger. Sid stood in stunned silence before him.

Chapter Four

Richard's Blunder

On both sides of the narrow street stood shabby apartment buildings and run-down houses. Richard checked the address on the slip of paper, then parked in front of an ugly building with an overgrown lawn and trash littering the sidewalk.

Richard smiled confidently as he strode up the walk and rang the bell for apartment 7. There was no sound, so he knocked.

Moments later, the door opened, revealing a disheveled Pam Messinger. Her eyes were heavy with sleep, her hair was a mess, and she pulled a cheap bathrobe tighter around her.

"What do you want?" Pam grumbled, staring at him.

"I called. Remember? I'm here to make you an offer," Richard said, smiling.

"You and that Fairgate—you're one and the same, aren't you? You gonna try to rape me, too?" she asked sleepily. She left the door open behind her and went to sit down at the kitchen table.

Richard followed her into the apartment. It was cluttered with ancient furniture, cheap throw rugs, records and magazines, clothing and empty boxes of cookies and donuts. "Nice place you got here," Richard said dryly.

"Oh, sure," Pam muttered, and pushed the table's contents—including an old bowl of cereal and curdled milk—onto the floor.

Richard jumped back as the milk splashed one leg of his expensive new slacks.

"Is it legal for you to talk to me like this?" Pam asked, bored.

"Sure. Mind if I sit?"

Pam shrugged. "If you can find a place."

The lawyer glanced around the room, and finally decided on the low bed that stuck out from the wall. He sank down on it until his hips were lower than his knees. Pam stood and looked at him.

"You're lying," she said. "It isn't legal for you to see or talk to me."

"Yes, it is," Richard said, in a pleasant tone. "Can we talk?"

She yawned. "We can try."

Dumb broad, Richard thought, looking at the girl. She was a mess, looked years older than the last time he'd seen her. She must be on drugs, he decided.

"You've really been friendly with the newspapers and television stations, haven't you?" Richard began.

"Yeah." She smiled. "See? That's me there, and there," she said, pointing to three newspaper articles tacked up on the wall.

"Yeah, well, you've embarrassed Sid Fairgate with your little game long enough, Miss Messinger. Of course, there's no danger of Mr. Fairgate being convicted, but—"

"Then why'd you call and ask if you could come over?" Pam asked slyly. "You're worried, all right, and I'll just bet Fairgate is, too."

Richard shrugged off the suggestion. "Look, Miss Messinger, Sid Fairgate is a respected Knots Landing businessman. He's very concerned about his reputation. Even though he'll be acquitted, this publicity will tarnish his future. People'll think back to when old Sid Fairgate was charged with rape. You should be happy—you've already managed to do this much damage."

Pam pouted. "I don't see you being so concerned about *me*. I have a reputation too, you know."

"Yeah, I'm learning," Richard said.

"What's that supposed to mean?" she asked, suddenly angry.

"Calm down, Pam. Look, all we need is for you to drop the charges against Sid. It won't make him a saint overnight, but it's a start." Richard paused and looked at her frankly. "We'd be prepared to reward you if you help us out on this."

Pam's eyes flickered with interest.

"Reward me? How?" She touched the tip of her tongue to her upper lip. "What do you have in mind?"

Avery smiled and, with difficulty, stood. He walked over to one corner of the studio apartment and gestured toward a cracked surfboard. "You like riding waves?"

"Sure," Pam said.

"A friend of mine owns a store that sells surfboards. He's a client of mine who owes me a favor. If you want, I'll give you his address and you could get yourself a new surfboard . . . or maybe a custom-made wet suit."

"What about scuba gear?" Pam asked, her eyes shining with excitement.

"Sure. He sells everything. You oughta stop by his store sometime." Richard pulled a pencil from his pocket and wrote the shop's address on the back of a donut box.

Pam watched him, still unconvinced. She cocked her head, then ran into the bathroom. As Richard stopped writing she reappeared. He did a double take.

She had slipped into jeans and a T-shirt. Pam slowly brushed her silky blond hair until it glowed in the late morning sunlight that flickered in through dusty windows. Pam was a changed young woman.

"What else?" she asked, staring at herself in a small hand mirror hanging beside the phone.

"Let's see," Richard said, scratching his cheek. Maybe she was buying it. He hoped so. "A friend of mine has a summer place right on the beach at Makaha," he said casually.

Pam's face brightened as she turned to him. "Makaha? In Hawaii?"

"Yeah," Richard said matter-of-factly. "They have some of the best waves in the world there."

"Don't I know it! I've wanted to go there for years!"

"Winter's coming up—and my friend's almost never there. He'd probably let you use his house for a few weeks."

Pam's smile suddenly faded. "How do I get over there?" she asked menacingly.

"I could probably get you a ticket. A travel agent I know owes—"

"First class," Pam said firmly.

"Well, okay," Richard said, nodding. "He might let you live there a month or two. How'd you like to move to Hawaii?"

Pam's smile blossomed. "Hawaii!" she exclaimed.

"That's just the beginning," Avery said. "I know lots of people in business, lots of them. It's my job to know them. And they all owe me. I keep it that way," he said, self-satisfied.

"Gee," Pam said, her eyes huge. "If I was living in Hawaii, or surfing every day and living in Malibu, maybe I wouldn't have time for some silly trial."

"Think so?" Richard asked guardedly.

"Yeah, but I wouldn't drop the charges until after I got the stuff. No sense in doing it

71

just for your big talk. Can you really get all that for me?" she asked wonderingly.

"Sure." He flashed a smile.

"Well, what do I have to do?"

"Just come down to the courthouse with me and sign one piece of paper. That's it." Avery paused. "I'll even drive."

"Yeah, okay, whatever," Pam said, and gazed into his eyes. "But not until *after*."

Richard smiled and nodded. "Great. I'll be in touch tomorrow." He started toward the door.

"Today!" Pam said. "I want the stuff today!"

"I'll do my best." Richard pushed the door open and closed it behind him, breathing in the comparatively fresh air outside. Leaving the oppressive apartment, Richard Avery—a representative of the prestigious law firm of Pincus, Simpson and Lyle—didn't feel a shred of guilt. He had just bribed a plaintiff into dropping the charges against his client, thus breaking every principal of the judicial system.

In fact, he was whistling happily as he unlocked his car.

Late Sunday night, Karen and Sid lay in their bed, waiting for sleep.

"Why does it feel like noon?" Karen asked.

"Because we're wide awake." Sid rustled the sheets gently as he rolled over onto his back.

Karen sighed, her cheek pressed against

the cool pillow. It smelled of perfume and salty tears. "We'll have to hire a criminal lawyer if you're indicted on Tuesday, Sid. Stan Loesser seems okay."

"But I thought he said Richard would be fine."

"Richard does his lawyering the way he does everything else—with the least possible amount of effort on his part. I'm sorry, Sid, but I truly don't trust him. And he hasn't done a thing about blowing apart that girl's ridiculous story. Besides, he said the girl would probably disappear. But she seems to be here for the duration."

"There's no way he could know what Pam was going to do, and I'm sure he's working on the case. He's just not telling us." He frowned. "It'll be tough, though. There are no witnesses, so it's her word against mine."

"But there have got to be holes some-where. She must have dropped her guard a few times. Richard isn't looking for Pam's mistakes. In fact, it looks like Richard isn't doing a damn thing."

"Hey, Karen," Sid said, touching her shoulder. "Richard's taking this very seriously."

"I just wish he'd use his head more, not his ego. I'm not sure—"

"Not sure about what?" he asked.

Karen shook her head. No reason to bring up her vague feelings. "It's not important. I just think Richard's not looking at this from the proper perspective."

"Honey, it'll be fine," Sid said assuredly.

"For you . . . or for her?"

Sid sat up in bed. "Karen, is it necessary for you to have the last word in every conversation we have?"

She looked at him, then smiled. "Yes." She rose and walked to the bathroom.

"I knew it," he said with a grin.

"You win." She pulled the door shut, cutting off any further remarks.

Richard was standing on his head beside his bed, his pajamed legs projecting up from the triangle formed by his hands and head.

Laura sat in bed, reading "Make Your First Million in Real Estate."

"Nothing like a good handstand to get your blood circulating," Richard said, still upside down.

His wife set her book down on the blanket. "How's the case for Sid going?" she asked, watching Richard's legs sway in the air.

"Fine, just fine," Richard said, and fell silent.

Laura sighed, pushed an old postcard from Rio into the book to mark her place, and set it on the nightstand. "That's not good enough for me, Richard. Talk to me. Tell me what you're doing, how the case is going."

"Fine, Laura. It's going fine." He dropped his feet down to the floor and sprang up, his hair flowing wildly around his head.

Laura frowned and turned off the light. "Let's just go to sleep," she said, rolling over on her side away from her husband.

She felt him climb into bed beside her, then waited tensely for the familiar creak that signalled he was reaching for her.

"Don't even try," she said, seconds before his hand touched her shoulder.

Richard sighed. "Sometimes you can be a real pain, Laura. You know that?"

She flung the covers back, jumped up from the bed, grabbed her robe and book and walked out of the room.

Her husband yawned, staring after her for a moment. He looked at the empty bed beside him, then stretched out so that his body monopolized the entire bed. He waited for his wife's return, and her inevitable reaction. He waited so long, in fact, that he fell asleep.

Richard woke when he felt himself being pushed by a pair of hands—and suddenly he was rolling off the bed and onto the floor.

"Hey!" he said. "I was sleeping!"

"Well, don't bother getting back in bed!" Laura screamed. "I'm not sleeping with you tonight, Richard. Not tonight or any night!" She pulled off her robe and threw it on a chair.

Richard watched her from his position on the bedroom floor. "Fine," he muttered wearily.

Laura lay down on the bed.

In the darkness Richard listened until her breathing grew deep and measured. Then gingerly he crept into bed beside her. This wasn't one of the best nights to bug the old lady, he decided, and smiled as he looked at her sleeping figure.

Richard wondered if he'd get any sleep that night.

"Give it to me!" Olivia yelled, grabbing the book from her brother's tiny hands.

"No! *I'm* reading it!" Brian wrenched it from his sister, then smiled wickedly.

"Mom!" Olivia cried, turning to her mother, who sat in the Fairgates' living room, watching her children disinterestedly.

"Olivia, stop screaming," Abby said quietly.

"But, *Mom!*"

"Quiet down!" Abby yelled, then stood and walked over to her children. Brian looked up at her, smiling sweetly, the book lying in his hands.

"Thank you!" Olivia said, and snatched the prize from her brother.

"She stole my book!" Brian howled.

"Brian! Olivia!" Abby exploded. "If you don't *both* keep quiet, you'll spend the rest of the afternoon upstairs. Is that clear?"

The children nodded. Brian glanced over at the book, which Olivia held tightly in her hands.

"Don't even think of trying that, Brian," Abby said.

The boy looked up, wide-eyed. "Trying what?"

"Look, I just can't take you kids fighting

this afternoon. I need some quiet, and I'm sure Karen and Sid do, too. We're guests here, so no more yelling. Okay?"

Brian tackled Olivia, sending her sprawling into a cushioned chair. The girl laughed, rolled off the chair and onto the carpet.

"Give it back!" Brian cried.

Abby threw up her hands as the door bell rang. She walked to the door and opened it.

"Abby!" Val said. "Is everything all right? I heard all that screaming outside . . ." Val peered inside.

"Come on in," the blonde said wearily, and indicated her children with a limp hand. "It's just youthful energy at work again."

Val smiled. "I wish I had half the energy that they do."

"How's Gary?" Abby asked, closing the door and leading Val into the living room. She eyed the woman curiously.

"He's fine, I guess. He just—"

"Gary keeps in shape, I've noticed," Abby said, lifting an eyebrow.

Val laughed warily. "Yes, Gary has always been pretty active." She smiled and looked at the screaming children. "Do you mind if I give it a try?"

Abby frowned, then shrugged. "Why not? Be my guest. I'll call the paramedics, just in case."

Val laughed and touched Abby's shoulder gently. She went over to the pair of children who looked ready for battle.

Olivia held the book firmly by one cover. Before she could clutch it to her chest, Brian took hold of the other cover and tugged on it. The volume split down the middle, sending both children tumbling to the carpet.

"Well!" Val said quietly.

Both children glanced up at her from the floor.

"Is that a nice thing to do to Diana's book?" she asked gently.

Olivia looked earnestly at Val, then at Abby, then at the book. She shook her head.

"What about you, Brian? What do you think?"

The boy touched his finger to his upper lip, then gently moved his head from side to side.

"Would you like it if Diana treated your books that way?" Val asked in the same gentle tone. She placed her hands on her knees and knelt before them. "I'm sure Diana won't be mad, since it was an accident. But if you had shared the book it would still be in one piece, and you wouldn't have to go tell Diana that you ripped up her book."

Brian swallowed and dropped his half of the book.

Val's smile broadened. "Now," she said in her lilting Southern voice, "I want you to apologize to each other and play *together*."

"But—" Brian started stubbornly.

"Shh." Val shook her finger. "You play now. Isn't it more fun when two play?"

Olivia frowned. "Play what?"

"Anything. Go figure out something to do while I talk with your mother, okay?"

Olivia nodded.

"Okay," Brian said reluctantly. He walked out to the backyard and Olivia trailed off after him.

"What do you want to play, Brian?" Olivia asked as she followed him.

"Cops and robbers," he said.

Val looked after them, grinning. "Sometimes they just need a few words of encouragement."

Abby stared at her for a moment. "What?"

Val couldn't mistake the look of anger on Abby's face. "I mean, you've been tired and worried—"

"I know what you're saying."

"Abby, I didn't mean—"

She sighed. "I'm sorry, Val. I thought things would be so much easier after the divorce. But it's harder than ever."

The other woman was silent.

"Well, it's been great talking with you, but I've got some calls to make," Abby said, glancing pointedly at the door.

Val started to leave. "Abby, they're wonderful children. I certainly didn't mean—"

But Abby was no longer listening. She had closed the door, and Val found herself all alone.

Richard ducked into the executive men's

washroom in the office building that housed Pincus, Simpson and Lyle. He checked his hair in the mirror, straightened his gray tie, and picked two specks of lint off his light blue coat. He looked quite respectable, he decided.

He felt slightly queasy at the thought of his upcoming meeting with Warren William Simpson, one of the law firm's founders. Simpson had the reputation of being very unapproachable; he was known for his impatience and condescending air.

Richard left the washroom and walked down the hallway to the last office on the end: the inner sanctum, the office of the holiest of holies—Warren William Simpson.

No secretary sat behind the desk in the outer office, so Richard cleared his throat and knocked on Simpson's door.

"Come in," a voice thundered.

Richard opened the door and walked into the panelled office, smiling nervously. He took a deep breath, trying to calm himself. "Good morning, sir," he said.

"Yes, quite," Simpson replied briskly. The man was perhaps sixty, his aging face showing the effects of years of law practice and hard work. He sat at his desk reading the newspaper, only his eyes and the top of his white-haired head visible.

He dropped the paper onto the desk. Richard looked down at it and grimaced. It was open to the article about Sid—and that ghastly picture.

"This is a rather unpleasant case, don't you think?" Simpson didn't look up at Avery.

"Not as bad as the paper's making it out to be," Richard said.

"No?" Simpson glanced at him for a moment, then turned his attention to the window.

"I live next door to Sid Fairgate. I got a call from him the night it happened and, well, as a favor to him I'm taking the case."

"I see. There won't be a fee?"

Richard sighed. "I suppose not. The man's my neighbor and I've known him for some time."

Simpson shook his head. "That can cause problems. If you don't charge a client a fee, how can he fire you?" The man laughed harshly, then fell silent.

Richard laughed along with Simpson, then abruptly stopped. What was he doing here? Why had Simpson called him to his office?

"Mr. Avery, you're one of our newer employees, aren't you?"

"That's right, Mr. Simpson."

"I see. Mr. Avery, if you feel that you are in need of assistance in this criminal case, please don't hesitate to give Mr. Hanover a call. He's available, and would be pleased to help you."

"Don Hanover?" Richard asked uneasily.

"Yes, of course," Simpson said, smiling. "He practiced criminal law for ten years in the L.A. area before he came to us."

Richard smiled. "I didn't know that.

Thanks for the offer, sir, but I think I can handle this myself."

"Oh?" Simpson's voice rose.

"I'm confident Mr. Fairgate will never be indicted, let alone convicted. The plaintiff is obviously of dubious reliability, while Sid Fairgate's reputation has always been above reproach."

"So that's how you're defending him? The contrast in characters?"

"Yes. But I have some other potentially rewarding tricks up my sleeve."

Simpson leaned forward and folded his hands on his desk. "What tricks?"

Richard smiled. "Too early to tell you for sure. But you can trust me, Mr. Simpson."

Simpson shrugged. "Fine, Mr. Avery. But don't forget—whether Mr. Fairgate pays you a fee or not, you still represent this firm."

"I won't let you down, sir," Richard said confidently.

Simpson frowned. "Good. Best of luck, then, Avery. That's all." He lifted the paper and began reading it as Richard hurriedly left the office.

Once outside Avery stomped through the outer office to the elevator. He felt his anger mounting the farther he got from Simpson's office.

He wouldn't let them do it to him again. They'd already ruined his chances twice before, but never again. Damn that Simpson! he fumed.

He punched the elevator's down button

and paced before the sleek metal doors. He wouldn't share a case with anyone, ever again. He was a competent lawyer and could handle a tricky case, make some media time, and establish his career as a fantastic lawyer.

In a few years, he would be living a life of luxury. A few big cases a year—making him, say, two or three million each—and he'd spend the rest of the time lying around the pool or travelling around the world in his jet, discovering the joys of women from Paris to Peru.

Richard smiled as the elevator doors opened. He stepped inside and pushed the button for the second floor. He'd win this rape case—not for Sid or the firm, but for himself. He'd make a name in this town. It would be the trial of the century.

Avery felt the elevator slow and stop on his floor as he planned how he'd spend his first million.

Walking out onto the second floor, Avery headed to his office, a secret grin on his lips.

Ginger clutched the phone in her hand. Kenny! What was he doing calling her at work? She turned away from the busy teachers' lounge at school and lowered her voice. "What do you want?" she asked. Behind her, teachers sat drinking coffee and chatting.

"To talk to you," Kenny said.

"I told you not to call—"

"I knew you had your break now and

thought I'd catch you in the lounge," Kenny said. "When can I see you again?"

Ginger shivered. "Never. I don't want to see you again, Kenny. Can't you understand that? How many times do I have to tell you?"

"What's that?" Kenny said. "I can't hear you, honey."

"Don't call me honey!" Ginger said.

The conversation in the room died down a bit, making Ginger blush. "I can't talk right now, Kenny," she hissed into the phone.

"Okay, then when?"

Ginger sighed. "I don't know. Call me some other time. Or better yet, don't call me at all." She hung up the phone and turned to face her fellow teachers.

Not one of them was paying attention to her. Everyone was listening to an obscene joke being told by Mr. Ackerman, the chemistry teacher.

Ginger walked out of the room into the brilliant sunshine and fresh air of the school's courtyard. Why wouldn't Kenny stop bothering her? What did he want? She wouldn't get back together with him, not after she'd caught him with that woman. She closed her eyes.

Eventually, Kenny would give up and she'd finally be at peace. How long he held out before that time was anyone's guess.

Chapter Five
Under the Gun

Monday morning, Pam Messinger sat in her run-down apartment, humming happily as she looked around the tiny room.

A shiny new surfboard leaned against one wall. Next to the board hung a full wet suit that she had picked up yesterday afternoon.

Several pairs of new jeans and four pretty blouses hung on rusty hangers in her tiny closet—all thanks to Richard Avery's generosity. If she held out a little longer, Pam thought, she might get everything she'd ever needed—or wanted.

Then Pam's face darkened. Her mother believed her rape story. What would she think when Pam changed her mind about testifying? Would she let Pam do it?

The girl shrugged. Her mother spent so little time in the cramped apartment, preferring the warm bedrooms of strangers, that it didn't really matter. Pam could always leave for Hawaii and live in that guy's place at Makaha. She smiled. Lots of rich men on the Islands. Maybe she could get a couple to take care of her.

The front door flew open. The knob banged against the wall, sending a small shower of plaster to the dirty floor. Pam looked up in dismay.

"Pam? You home?" Selma Messinger said as she walked into the apartment, dressed in a shocking pink polyester pant suit. She held a bag of groceries in her arms. "I picked up a—what the hell's going on here?" Selma demanded. "What's all this stuff?" She hurried over to the table, set the bag down, and surveyed the room.

"It's mine," Pam said. "A friend of mine gave it to me."

Selma raised a bushy eyebrow. "Oh yeah? What'd you have to do to get it?"

"Nothing," Pam said, feigning innocence. "He's a rich lawyer and he knows how to make me happy."

Selma smirked. "Yeah? How's that?"

"He buys me anything I want." She grinned. "He's even sending me on a trip to Hawaii!" she said, smiling broadly.

"Wait just a minute, young lady!" Selma said, holding up her hand in warning. Her body shook gently as she pushed herself into the chair. "What kind of 'friend' is this? No one spends thousands of dollars on a seventeen-year-old girl," she said, shaking her head.

"*He* does. His name's Rick. I like him."

"Rick?" Selma mused. She strummed the armrest with bright pink fingernails. "You said he's a lawyer?"

Pam thought quickly. "That's right." She looked at her mother. She was getting too close to the truth.

Selma looked at the merchandise again, then at her daughter. "Has that pervert's lawyer been over here to see you yet?" she asked. "I just bet he'll be by sooner or later."

"Well, as a matter of fact . . ."

"I thought so." She smiled. "I'm sorry I was away last night again. I'm over that fight we had. And I just want you to know that I'm gonna be here for my daughter."

Pam smiled weakly.

"I was visiting an old friend of your father's—Mason. Do you remember him?" Selma looked at her expectantly.

"Sure," Pam said with a sigh. "I remember."

"Well, never mind about that now. So, Fairgate's lawyer came by to see you? Pam, did he give you all this stuff?" Her eyes narrowed suspiciously.

"Well, maybe," the girl admitted.

"He's trying to bribe us!" she said, and slapped her knee. "That lawyer's as much of a pervert as Sid Fairgate! How *dare* he think he could bribe us? What do you think you'll do?" she asked. "Take a little more of his stuff, then turn it over to the D.A.?"

"Actually, I was thinking—"

"That's great! It's a sure thing we'll win. It'll show how desperate Sid Fairgate is, that he'd have his attorney try to bribe you." Selma's face glowed with joy. "You're pretty smart sometimes, kid, you know that?"

"Yeah," Pam said, and smiled back. She'd been spared her mother's wrath. But at what price? No trip to Hawaii, and she'd have to give everything back. She frowned. Couldn't she get rid of her mother for a while? If only she'd go out for a few hours, Avery could come by, take her to sign the legal papers, and drop her off at the airport. She'd have to pack, but that wasn't—

"I just want you to know," Selma said, interrupting her thoughts. "I'll be staying here from now on—morning, noon and night. My little girl needs her mother now. She's going through a tough time. All my gentleman friends will just have to spend their nights alone for a while."

"Great," Pam said, watching her dreams disappear.

"Why don't you call that pervert lawyer right now? Tell him to come over. When he gets here, we'll show him we can't be bought with no lousy presents," Selma said, grinning at her daughter. "Right, baby?"

Pam sighed. She was caught. "Right," she said, and walked to the phone.

"Relax, honey," Sid said to Karen as they ate lunch. Their kids had already finished and had gone upstairs to their rooms. They seldom ventured outside to play since the newspaper article. "The preliminary hearing's tomorrow. I'm sure everything will be fine."

"What if it isn't?" Karen shook her head. "Sid, we have to start making contingency plans, just in case the worst thing happens."

"But I'd rather think positively, sweetheart," Sid said, and took a bite of his egg salad sandwich.

"Fine. You think positively, I'll make plans. Just in case the girl shows up for the hearing and convinces the judge that you're guilty. I know that won't happen, but—"

"Then don't worry about it, okay, Karen?" He picked up his glass of milk, then set it down quickly. It shook in his hands, and he didn't want her to see that. "Everything will be fine."

Karen smiled bravely at him, then stood and walked around to him. She placed a tender kiss on his cheek. "Hang in there, tiger," she whispered.

Pam had slipped into a pair of jeans and a bright red blouse by the time the door bell rang.

"Okay, Pam, let me hide in the bathroom until the time is right." Selma slipped inside the tiny room and pulled the door closed.

Pam waited a moment, then shouted, "It's open!"

Richard Avery walked in.

"Oh, it's you," she said.

"Something wrong? Didn't you get the stuff? Oh, I see you did get it. Nice surfboard, Pam. You're some shopper, aren't you?"

"I do my best." Pam looked at him sincerely.

"Well, time to get down to the police station." Richard's voice was carefully light in tone.

Selma Messinger pushed open the bathroom door and strode out into the cluttered apartment. "She's not leaving this house!"

"Oh, did I forget to tell you?" Pam asked Richard. "I live with my mother. She's just been gone for a few days, staying with an old friend."

Selma rested her hands on her hips. "What're you trying to do to my daughter?"

"Nothing," Richard said.

"You're trying to bribe Pam, aren't you? Bribe her so that she won't land your friend in jail. Isn't that right?"

"Wait a minute," Richard said, shaking his head. "Did I miss something here?" His voice was smooth. "If you're implying that I bought and paid for all this stuff for Pam, you're wrong. I got her discounts at the stores because I have friends. But that's all—just discounts."

"Sure," Selma said, smiling knowingly. "And what about that trip to Hawaii? Do you have friends with the airlines, too?"

Richard smiled. "As a matter of fact—"

"Shut up!" the woman roared. "I don't

believe you. I suggest you get out of here. Now!"

"Wait a minute," Richard said, losing his mask of composure.

"You're paying my daughter to lie for your friend. Well, mister, we aren't liars!"

Richard chuckled nervously as he watched his case fall apart. "Your daughter sure is," he said. "She's had lots of practice lately."

"Hey! I resent that!" Pam snapped.

"Boy, you're some kind of people, you rich folks." Selma glared at him in disgust. "Sid Fairgate tries to rape my daughter, then sends you over to buy her silence."

"Hey, this was only business," Richard said, pointing to the surfboard.

"So's pimping." She sneered at him.

"Mom," Pam said, uneasily.

She turned to her daughter. "What is it? You're not having second thoughts, are you?" she asked darkly.

"No, but—"

"Good. Sid Fairgate almost raped you, right?"

Pam was silent for a moment, then nodded.

"Well then, I don't see—"

"Mrs. Messinger," Richard said, "if you'd just—"

"No!" the woman shrieked. "You and your friends may be richer than we are, but we're tough. We can see this thing through."

"But, Mom!" Pam pleaded. "A trip to Hawaii! Two trips, maybe!"

Selma's eyes searched her daughter's face. Pam flushed. She'd tripped up again, spoken before she'd thought about what she was going to say.

"What did you say, young lady?" Selma demanded.

Pam's cheeks were burning. "Nothing."

"A trip to Hawaii's not worth losing what little respect you and I may still have for ourselves. We won't sell out!"

Richard shook his head. "That's not what's happening here. This is simply a solution to a grave misunderstanding, a solution that is beneficial to all parties involved. It isn't selling out or taking a bribe. It's like plea bargaining, in a way."

Selma nodded. "Fine. Bargain with someone else." She smiled wickedly and turned to Pam. "This trial's gonna make us famous, Pam! We won't hide anything— we'll go out in public and brag about the skeletons in our closets. Just because we're not living in a nice neighborhood doesn't give Fairgate any right to rape you, Pam! So forget it, mister. There won't be any bribes, or trips to Hawaii. We'll make history with this case. Hell, I can't wait until it starts!"

Richard was starting to sweat, but he tried to remain in control. "This isn't a game, Mrs. Messinger. This isn't television. Trials can be boring, unpleasant, or worse—they can make you see the truth about people that you'd probably rather not see." He glanced at Pam, who stood next to the surfboard, one hand sliding down its smooth surface.

"There's no truths about Pam—good or bad—that I don't know about," Selma said firmly. "Isn't that right, Pam?"

"Sure, Mom."

"I can't stand this dump." Selma looked around the apartment. "Compared to this place, a warm courtroom'll be a palace. So take your bribes and get out!" Selma walked over to the surfboard, lifted it in her strong arms, and threw it at the rapidly departing Richard Avery. He made it out the door seconds before the heavy fiberglass board clattered to the floor behind him.

"I don't want to see your face again, mister! Not until the trial!" Selma stepped back into her apartment and turned to her daughter.

"Thanks a lot, Mother," Pam murmured bitterly.

"You weren't gonna lie for that man's money, were you?"

Pam laughed. "A house in Hawaii? At Makaha?" She shrugged. "I'd do almost anything for that. But I knew in the end I'd give in. You just happened to be here to do it for me. That's all." She smiled.

"Sometimes you worry me, Pam," Selma said. "I know it hasn't always been easy for you, but I tried to do things right raising you. I was hoping you wouldn't grow up the wrong way."

"I didn't, Mom." Pam stared forlornly at the shiny new surfboard. She sighed.

* * *

In a quiet courtroom, Sid, Karen and Richard sat before the judge. On the other side of the room, Selma and Pam Messinger watched the robed man with equal interest. Between the two groups paced the D.A., a handsome black man with a thin moustache.

Karen gripped Sid's hand as the judge read over the last few notes concerning the trial. He finally looked up.

Karen caught her breath. *Here it comes,* she thought. *Now we'll know . . .*

"In the opinion of this court, probable cause for proceeding with this case does exist."

Karen paled. Her fingers gripped Sid's frantically.

"This court recommends that William Sidney Fairgate, the defendant, be bound over to stand trial in Superior Court on the charges of assault, assault with attempt to rape, and contributing to the delinquency of a minor." The judge scowled behind his thick glasses. "You'll be informed as to date and court." He banged his gavel. "Dismissed."

Sid suddenly released Karen's hand. She turned to him, questioningly, but was surprised to see no emotion on Sid's face. He was in shock.

They rose as the judge did. Karen felt eyes on her, and she turned to face the Messingers. Pam's mother, Selma, smiled triumphantly. Beside her the girl sat calm, seemingly bored.

After staring back at Karen for a moment, Selma made a "thumbs down" gesture.

Karen leaned closer to her husband. "Honey," she whispered. "Are you all right?"

Sid shook his head. "I can't believe it."

Karen grabbed his arm and looked at Richard, who hastily gathered his papers and stuffed them in his briefcase. He was obviously in a hurry to leave.

Avery glanced up and caught Karen's stare. "Now look, Karen, there's no need to worry."

She laughed harshly. "Don't tell me that! When *will* it be time, Richard? When should I worry? As they're locking Sid up and throwing away the key?"

"Karen, let me—"

"No, Richard, I won't let you do anything!" she said in a forced whisper. "And I won't listen to you. You told us this wouldn't happen, remember? You *promised* us!"

"I'm sorry I exaggerated," Richard said. "I wanted to make you feel better."

"Yeah? Well, how do you think I feel right now, Richard?"

"Karen, there's no case against Sid," he said quietly. The room had emptied out. "Pam can't possibly win. Put any thoughts of that out of your mind."

"This judge thinks differently. 'Probable cause.' I don't believe it!"

"Karen, calm down!" Richard begged.

"I will not calm down!" Karen lowered her

voice. "My husband's reputation and good name are in danger, and you won't help!"

"It's a formality, that's all," Richard explained helplessly.

"I can't believe you'd gamble with Sid's whole life this way. Why can't you be upfront about what you're doing? What *have* you been doing, anyway, Richard?"

He hung his head, desperate and confused. Then he glanced at Sid. "Hey, pal," he whispered tentatively.

Sid didn't look up at him.

"I may not know what you've been doing, Richard," Karen said. "But I know what you've done!"

Avery looked away and slid his briefcase from the table. He could not bear to face Karen's painful accusations—nor Sid's silent ones—a moment longer.

Soaps & Serials™
Fans!

 Order the *Soaps & Serials™* books you have missed in this series.

 Collect other *Soaps & Serials™* series from their very beginnings.

 Give *Soaps & Serials™* series as gifts to other fans.

...see other side for ordering information

From Pioneer Communications Network, Inc.

You can now order previous titles of *Soaps & Serials*™ Books by mail!

Just complete the order form, detach, and send together with your check or money order payable to:

Soaps & Serials™
120 Brighton Road, Box 5201
Clifton, NJ 07015-5201

- - - - - - - - - - - - - - - - - - - -

Please <u>circle</u> the book #'s you wish to order:

The Young and The Restless	1	2	3	4	5	6	7
Days of Our Lives	1	2	3	4	5	6	7
Guiding Light	1	2	3	4	5	6	7
Another World	1	2	3	4	5	6	7
As The World Turns	1	2	3	4	5	6	7
Dallas™	1	2	3	4	5	6	7
Knots Landing™	1	2	3	4	5	6	7
Capitol™	1	2	3	4	NOT AVAILABLE		

Each book is $2.50 ($3.50 in Canada).

Total number of books
circled _____ × price above = $ _____ .

Sales tax (CT and NY residents only) $ _____ .

Shipping and Handling $ _____ .95

Total payment enclosed $ _____ .
(check or money orders only)

Name _____

Address _____ Apt# _____

City _____

State _____ Zip _____

Telephone (_____) _____
Area code   KI. 7

Chapter Six

From Bad to Worse

As Eric Fairgate pushed his bicycle home, it made an irritating thumping noise as the flat tires flopped against the pavement.

He should have known better than to try to go to the beach. After all, it was open season on the Fairgate family in Knots Landing.

A wave of anger passed over him, then subsided. In its place the boy felt only shame and anger. Why didn't he know what was going on? Why wouldn't anyone tell him how long things would be like this?

He turned past the bus stop and onto Seaview Circle. He stared straight ahead and cut directly across the sidewalk to his house.

Wearily, Eric dropped his bike in the garage and went inside. As he entered the kitchen, he heard voices in the living room. Great, he thought. His parents were giving parties while his father was under arrest for trying to rape a girl. He shook his head and ducked into the living room.

Karen turned as her son entered the living room. "Hi, Eric."

He mumbled a response and ran up the stairs to his bedroom.

"Look, Karen, I know what I'm doing. I'm the lawyer," Richard Avery said. He sat beside his wife on the couch.

Karen put an arm around her husband. "What was that you were saying before Eric walked through?"

"The same thing I'm saying now." He turned to Sid. "It's my fondest wish that your wife would leave the legalities to me. I'm the expert," he said and smiled smugly.

"I'd be glad to, but you won't tell me what you're doing!" Karen said a trifle loudly.

Richard nodded and reached down to retrieve his briefcase. "You already know most of it, Karen," he said, fumbling with some papers inside the briefcase. "I've got that private investigator doing background research on the girl."

"You're *paying* someone to discover her seamy past? Just read the headlines," she said sarcastically. "She's been bragging about it for days now. She's trying to appear honest, letting everyone know exactly what her background is."

"It won't work," Richard said. "She's swatting at flies in the dark."

Karen shook her head. "She's already got the media in the palm of her hand. She's become a kind of folk hero to the people in this town."

"I wouldn't say that, not quite," Sid interrupted.

"She's yelling 'I'm a tramp!' at the top of her lungs. And meanwhile, every journalist in town has convicted Sid while we sit here talking about how it can't happen—not to our Sid! Why don't you at least have a criminal lawyer working with you, someone who knows his way around this kind of case?"

"Karen, if it comes to that, I'm sure Richard will be glad to talk to someone—" Laura began.

"Is that right, Richard?" Karen asked skeptically.

"Honey, please," Sid said.

"No, it's all right, Sid," Richard murmured. "Karen's just upset."

"I'm not upset!" she thundered. "I'm scared to death—for all of us."

"You can set your mind at ease, Karen."

"Don't start that again, Richard," Laura warned.

"No. What you don't know is that I've got an ace up my sleeve."

Karen looked at him, exasperated. "Why haven't any of us heard about this ace? Why are you being so secretive about everything?"

"It's my style," Richard said with a smile. "I took a chance and invited the prosecutor to lunch. We talked. He's willing to make a deal."

"What kind of deal?" Sid asked, sitting

forward, tapping his foot nervously.

"He's willing to throw out the charges of contributing to the delinquency of a minor and assault with attempted rape."

"What does that leave me to take a dive on?" Sid asked hesitantly.

"Harassment and assault."

"But there's no proof!" Karen cried. "And Sid's innocent. I can't believe you're even considering plea bargaining, Richard. I really can't! That's practically admitting guilt."

"You've got that wrong, Karen." He lifted an eyebrow as if daring her to question him. "It just makes sense here. Sometimes doing things the normal way is too messy, expensive and dangerous to honest citizens who get into the wrong place at the wrong time."

"You're just giving up?" Karen asked, incredulous. "What about you, Sid? What do you think?"

"Well—"

Karen glared at Richard from across the coffee table. "Maybe if you'd spent some time on this case and taken it seriously, you might have something else to offer Sid!" she raged.

"Hey, Karen, that's uncalled for," Laura said. "How could any of us know that it would turn out this way?"

Karen glanced at the other woman, her eyes wild, but she said nothing.

"Karen." Sid touched her shoulder gently. "In the end, it has to come down to realities. I mean, we have to face the facts. I blindly offered the wrong girl a ride, thinking I was saving her from mortal danger. Now she's trying to ruin my life. I'm in over my head here. There's too much at stake. There's only one thing I can do."

"Exactly!" Richard said, jumping to his feet. "I'll call the prosecutor and tell him we accept his offer."

Sid laughed. "Slow down, Richard. I'm afraid you don't understand."

"I hope not," Karen said, her face pale.

Sid smiled patiently. "If Pam gets away with this, not only will *my* life be ruined, but she'll be able to go out and do it again and again. That's too much responsibility for me."

"Who cares about responsibility?" Richard asked. "Think about your responsibility to your family. This lets you off easy. In comparison with the alternative—there *is* no alternative."

Sid sighed.

"Look, maybe after a good night's sleep you'll be more clear-headed. Call me in the morning," the lawyer told him.

"I am clear-headed! Aren't I getting through to you, Richard? The answer is no. I'm innocent, and I'm going to fight against every one of that girl's lies."

The lawyer let out a slow sigh. "Okay, but you're swimming upstream."

"Daddy!" Diana cried from the doorway. Unnoticed, she had been listening in on their conversation. "Why don't you go ahead and do whatever Mr. Avery tells you to?"

He looked solemnly at his daughter. "Impossible."

"But why?"

"I just told you and everyone else in this room why."

"But those terrible lies that girl's been saying—she's ruining us! Our whole family!"

Sid frowned. "Exactly why I can't and won't compromise at this point! I have to prove that it isn't true, even though the law isn't supposed to work against me all the way."

Diana sighed. "I guess so. But isn't it ever going to get better? Won't it ever be over, I mean all over?"

Sid was silent.

Richard cleared his throat as he rose. "See you later, Sid," he said on his way to the door.

Laura looked at Karen. "Richard'll do everything he can," she said, and followed him out.

"That's what scares me," Karen whispered as the door closed. "I don't know what that man is capable of." She turned to Sid. "I'm just so worried, honey."

"I know," he said with a sigh. "I've never been so scared in my life, Karen."

"Richard! Richard!" Laura called as he hurried away from the Fairgates'.

Her husband was already halfway to the

sidewalk. He walked briskly toward their house, directly next door to Sid and Karen's home on Seaview Circle.

"What?" he asked irritably.

"Why not get some help with this case? It sounds reasonable to me."

"Laura, listen to me. It clearly comes down to a case of her word against his. The only way for the jury to decide the guilt or innocence of the defendant is by contrasting the characters of the two parties involved."

Laura hurried to keep up with her husband. "Okay," she said. "So?"

"So I have to find as much evidence as I can against her, to cast doubt on her veracity. I can call in upstanding citizens who'll swear up and down that Sid is the most moral person that ever walked the face of the earth—which is true, by the way. Sure, Pam Messinger's daring, outspoken, and riding the tails of a successful media campaign proclaiming her innocence. But tell me honestly, who do you think the jury will favor?"

Laura seemed somewhat taken aback. "Okay, honey," she said gently. "But wouldn't it be a good idea to ask your company—"

He shook his head vehemently. "No!"

"Why not?" Laura demanded.

Richard's fuse was running short. "Old man Simpson already called me into his office to talk about the case. He said I should call Don Hanover to see if he'd help me. I told him no way." He exhaled deeply.

"You what?"

"You'll never understand, will you? I'm drowning there, Laura, drowning in the shadows of the other bright, successful, newsworthy attorneys and their million dollar cases." He opened the front door and walked into his house. "I've had it. I can't do it any longer. But I figure, since Sid's case has been getting so much media coverage, a win—or a partial win—could help us *both* out. It could make my career."

Laura closed the door behind her. "Yeah, you're right. But if you lose, it'll ruin Sid's life."

He turned and looked at her for a moment, then shrugged and wandered off to the living room. "Great, Laura. You really know what I need to hear." He disappeared from her sight.

Diana held her books tightly to her chest as she walked to her locker, avoiding the occasional stares of her classmates. School had become a miserable experience since her father's name had shown up on the front page of the paper.

She kept her head low as she turned the corner, nearly at her locker. She didn't see the other student coming around the corner until they collided, sending Diana stumbling back. She dropped one of her books.

"Sorry, I—" the boy began, then looked up at Diana. His face paled. "Oh, I—I'm sorry,

Diana," he said, and backed away from her.

Diana threw the rest of her books to the floor, wanting to scream. But she thought better of it and stooped to pick up her belongings. She hurried to her locker and automatically dialed the combination.

Farther down the hallway, just out of sight, Diana heard two girls giggling and opening their own lockers.

"Why can't I ever remember my combination, Trish?" one of the voices said.

"Because you're brain damaged, Betsy. You always were and you always will be."

"That's not what Kevin said." Betsy's voice was suggestive.

"Kevin? You don't mean the guitar player from the rock group?"

"That's right!" Betsy giggled as she opened her locker. "I never thought he knew I existed. But then he came up to me yesterday and said he heard that I sang."

Diana dropped her books quietly into her locker. *Don't panic,* she told herself. *Everything's fine. Betsy must be lying or embellishing on the truth.* She searched for the books for her next class, but couldn't help overhearing the other girls' conversation.

"What do you mean, you know Mr. Fairgate?" Trish asked, gasping.

"Well, I do," Betsy said conspiratorially.

"Yeah? Go on!" Trish said eagerly.

"Well, one night he was taking Diana and me home. After a while, Mr. Fairgate told me Diana had a headache, so guess what he did?" Her eyes were flashing brightly.

"What?" Trish sounded breathless. "And why didn't you ever tell me this before?"

"You never asked. Anyway, he stopped by his house first and dropped Diana off, then drove me to my house."

Trish squealed. "You're *kidding!* You mean, you were all alone in the car with him?"

"That's right."

Stop it, Betsy! Diana thought. *Stop making up lies! My father never did that. You're just trying to impress Trish, the school beauty, because she's popular and has more friends than you do.*

"I can't believe this!"

"On the way to my house, Mr. Fairgate asked me all these personal questions. Things like, did I like bicycling, or camping in the mountains."

"No!" Trish giggled.

"Yeah. I figured he was serious, wanting to know if I liked to do those kinds of things, so I answered him. I never dreamed that he—"

"How could you?" Trish asked. "How could anyone?"

Lies! Diana wanted to scream. *You're lying!*

"Wait, there's more," Betsy said sinisterly. "Finally we got to my house and he offered to walk me to the door. I thought that was nice of him."

"Right, sure!"

"*Then* I did. *Now* I know better."

Diana sighed, and leaned against her locker door.

"Anyway, not one light in the house was

on as we walked up to it. I said, 'Doesn't look like my parents are home. We're alone.' "

"No!"

"Yes!"

Betsy's voice rose dramatically. "Mr. Fairgate said he should come into the house with me, just in case. After all, it was dark outside." Betsy paused. "So . . ."

"So?" Trish urged, eager for more.

"So I unlocked the door and he crept around the house, barely making a sound, like a thief."

Diana felt despair and disbelief as she listened to Betsy's story—yet she couldn't bring herself to walk away.

"He turned on all the lights, one by one, in almost every room of the house."

"And then?" Trish asked breathlessly.

"And then—nothing."

"Nothing!" She sounded disappointed.

"Hey, it's not my fault!" Betsy said, defensive. "Maybe he was afraid my parents would come back or something."

"Still, it's awful! You shouldn't have told me!" Trish said.

"Why not?" Betsy asked innocently.

"I have to spread this story around!"

"Trish, really?" Betsy asked, stunned.

"Come on, you know I do. This is too good to keep quiet about."

"Wait a minute, Trish." Betsy said. "I didn't tell you this so that you could tell everyone else."

"Why not? That's the way it works around

here. You should know—you've heard enough gossip about everyone else."

"That's true," Betsy said reluctantly.

"Probably even about me, right?" Trish said.

"Hey, back off, Trish!"

Diana heard a brief scuffle, then a raucous laugh. "Okay!" Trish said, laughing. "Just joking. Come on! If you want to hang out with me, you gotta play the games. Loosen up, Betsy, you're not a kid anymore." Trish paused a moment. "Or are you? I mean, just because Mr. Fairgate didn't do anything that night . . ."

Diana slammed her locker shut, leaving all her books inside, and ran to the bathroom. As she shot past the lockers she heard Betsy's voice.

"Anyway, I was so innocent then. I liked him more than any of my other friends' fathers, because he was the nicest. Can you believe I used to think that?"

The tears were streaming down her cheeks before Diana reached the privacy of the bathroom.

"Okay, forget it, guys!" Kevin Newsom's voice echoed in the empty auditorium. Assembled on the stage around him were his musicians. Lounging beside a four-foot tall amp was an attractive red-haired girl holding a sheet of music.

"Keep looking over the song until you're ready for us, okay, Mary?"

The girl looked up at Kevin and nodded. "Okay," she said, and smiled at him before lowering her gaze.

Kevin sighed. Auditioning girl singers for the group was a very mixed blessing. Mary was one of the blessings. He just hoped he could avoid confronting Diana Fairgate today. He didn't have the strength.

"Sorry I'm late," Diana said as she strode into the auditorium, her cheeks puffy, eyes slightly red. She walked onto the stage, then slowed her pace. She and Mary looked at each other icily for a moment, then the singer shrugged.

"Kevin?" Diana asked slowly.

"I'm sorry, Diana," Kevin said, not approaching her. "We—I—I mean, I thought you wouldn't, you know, be in the mood to sing with us. You know," he said, smiling awkwardly. *Why today?* he wondered miserably.

"So you're already looking for another girl singer? Boy, you sure don't waste any time, do you, Kevin? At least you could have asked me."

"Diana, you know the score. You're controversial." He frowned. "We're gonna try to go professional, get some gigs at clubs, dances, you know."

Diana shook her head, then turned and walked off the stage. She didn't look back as she left the auditorium.

Karen and Sid Fairgate sat in their living

room. "Well, that does it," Karen said firmly.

"That does what?" Sid asked.

"I'm sorry, but I'm calling Stan Loesser. I think it's come to that."

"Wait a minute. You know what that'd do to Richard?" Sid asked, his face filled with concern.

Karen shook her head. "I don't care what it does to Richard. I only care about you. With plea bargaining there's no way you can be vindicated in this. And I'm not going to let Richard do that to you!"

"Karen, the D.A. offered him the plea bargaining, and he had to let me know about it. That doesn't mean he's going to go through with it."

"I don't trust him. I'm not so sure he wouldn't manipulate—"

"Who? Me?" Sid asked, smiling.

"No, it's just that he's so, well, you know, *unorthodox*." Karen frowned. "That's not what I'm trying to say. Sleazy isn't quite right either."

"Karen!"

"I'm just afraid that you won't see what real danger you're in until it's too late to do anything about it. That's why I'm calling Stan Loesser," she said firmly. "I won't let you stop me, Sid. I mean it. I want to get his advice."

Brian and Olivia burst into the room, Brian tooting on his horn as his sister screamed at the top of her lungs.

Abby rushed into the room after them, out

of breath. "Brian, give that back to your sister!"

Karen noticed a small object in the boy's hand, but couldn't tell what it was.

"Hi, Karen," Abby said, looking up at her.

"Hello, Abby."

"Diana around? I was hoping she could watch the kids later tonight."

"She's supposed to be at a rehearsal until six or six-thirty," Karen said.

"Oh." She smiled. "Karen, you don't suppose you could—"

"I'm sorry, Abby. I love Brian and Olivia but I can't take much more of their energy."

"Hey, honey," Sid said. "We invited Abby here, remember?"

"Sid, if I can—" Abby began.

The front door swung open and Diana stormed into the living room. Her face was red and wet, her body tense with anger and frustration.

"What's wrong, sweetheart?" Karen asked anxiously.

Diana stopped at the foot of the stairs.

"You okay, honey?" Sid asked.

She turned to him. "Why couldn't you have just driven off that night? Why'd you have to stop for her?"

"Diana, you know the whole story," Karen said. "You've heard it many times."

"I know, but I haven't heard the most important part."

"And what's that?" Sid asked, confused.

Abby folded her arms before her and

111

watched with interest.

"I don't know *why* you let that teenaged sex fiend into your car at night. I know what you *told* me, but—"

"Diana! That's more than enough!" Karen yelled.

Sid reached for his daughter's hand but she pulled it away.

"Daddy, it's so sick! The way everybody's acting and the whole story and the newspaper articles and the news shows and everything! We'll never be the same again. No one will ever treat us like normal people again. *Ever!*" Diana raced up the stairs, in tears.

"Diana!" Karen cried, and started after her.

"No!" Sid said firmly. He grabbed Karen's arm. "I have to do this," he said. "I have to talk to her."

Karen bit her lower lip, then nodded. "You're right. I'm sorry, Sid."

His expression grim, Sid started up the stairs.

Chapter Seven
Time of Trial

Sid Fairgate stood before his daughter's door moments after her outburst. He paused, then knocked loudly.

"Sweetheart?"

No answer.

"Diana!"

"What?"

He opened the door and walked in. His daughter sat on her bed, beneath the bears, lions and other stuffed animals dangling from the wall above her. She was staring at the wall.

"Daddy, do we have to talk right now? I'm in no mood for a heart-to-heart, father-daughter session right now, or for any of your advice." She pouted.

"Advice?" Sid smiled. "What makes you think I'm going to give you advice? I'm no expert at this, you know. It's my first time. I don't know how you should act any more than I know how I should."

"Okay," she said reluctantly, and glanced up at him.

"I didn't come here to offer you advice, but to ask for your support. I feel like you're deserting the ship while it *seems* to be sinking."

"It *is* sinking, Daddy. If you knew the things I'm going through because of you—"

"I don't know. But I can tell you one thing, Diana. Whatever your life's been like these past few days, it's been just as hard—maybe even harder—for your mother and me. Don't forget, your mother has to sleep with me every night, while everyone thinks that her husband, the father of her children, raped a young girl."

"But—but—I'm falling apart!" Diana wailed.

"Really?" he asked. "Then you're not nearly as tough as I thought you were. It might get worse than this, you know. I may be convicted of a crime I didn't commit and be thrown in prison for a few years. Have you thought about that?"

"Of course I've thought about it!"

"Sure, you've thought about how it'll hurt *you*. But do you think this thing is happening to you alone? Ask your brothers, or your mother, or our neighbors."

"Daddy, I'm sorry," Diana sobbed, tears streaming down her cheeks. "Why'd this have to happen to us? To you?"

"I don't know, Diana." He frowned,

remembering that fateful night. "There was a girl your age on the street. A man started roughing her up, so I backed my car up and opened the door. She got in, we drove away, and I was happy I'd saved a young woman from a lot of trouble. Then she gave me more trouble than I could ever have imagined."

"Are you sorry you picked her up?" Diana asked, drying her eyes on her sleeve.

Sid hesitated. "Yes and no. I'm not sorry I tried to save her, but I'm sorry I got myself into this mess. That's the real tragedy of it all. From now on I'll be less likely to stop and help someone out on the road with a flat, or hitchhiking late at night on a lonely street. Most of those people are okay out there, but the ones who aren't . . ." Sid sighed. "They'll throw you to the lions before you know what hit you. We'll probably all turn into cynics, thinking the worst of people, never lending a hand. I hate the idea. You should hate it, too."

Diana frowned, and said nothing.

"So think about that, honey. Get rid of this pride and self-pity before you come back downstairs, Diana. You and every other member of this family have to stand together with me on this thing, or I'm lost." His frown deepened. "We're all lost."

Diana glanced at him but remained silent, her face reflective.

He stroked her hair and left her room, closing the door quietly behind him.

* * *

Sid sipped his coffee as he stood in the corner of the Knots Landing Motors repair shop. Fewer than half the service bays were in use, and his crew had had an easy day with the reduced work load. An employee passed by as Sid stood drinking his coffee.

"Hi, Bill," Sid said.

The man waved curtly and walked on.

Several women stood outside in the sun, whispering to each other and staring at Sid. They'd obviously seen his picture in the paper or on television. He looked at them directly, sending them scurrying out of sight.

He set down his coffee cup and returned his attention to the engine he'd been building for the last several years. But he knew his heart wasn't in his work. He sighed and bent over it.

"Will you sign this, please?" his secretary asked suddenly.

Sid jumped, startled, then laughed at his reaction. "Sorry, I'm a little edgy today." He took the clipboard and pen from the woman, who stood smiling politely. He signed his name and handed the clipboard back to her.

"Thank you," she said brusquely, and was gone.

Sid washed his hands and walked into the showroom, then into Gary Ewing's office. The handsome blond man was talking on the phone, his face tense.

"Look, you don't believe everything you read in the papers, do you?" he asked as Sid walked in. Gary shrugged at his boss and returned to his conversation. "I know. Look, if you're worried about that, we won't put Knots Landing Motors on the license plate holders for the cars." He paused. "Look, Mr. Regula, you ordered five cars for your firm. We've gone to great expense—"

Sid shook his head sadly.

"Hey, Regula, when did you turn into a judge? That girl's lying and everyone knows it. What do you mean, she's telling the truth? Come over here and say that to me in person, bud, and I'll push your face in with my fist!" Ewing slammed the receiver down.

"Had many calls like that today?" Sid asked lamely.

"That was the second one," Gary said. "But Kramer Courier Service is suddenly having second thoughts."

"Great." Sid glanced at his watch. "It's only two-thirty. We might not go broke until dark."

Gary ran his hand through his hair. "We're not that bad off. And it's not just us—the car industry's in a decline. Did you say it was two-thirty? That Jaycee meeting's at three." He rose and walked to the door.

"It slipped my mind completely," Sid said, "Let me take off these overalls and I'll be ready to go with you."

Gary turned back to Sid. "Sorry, Sid, but I let them know I'd do the lecture."

Sid sighed. "Whose idea was that? Yours or theirs?"

Ewing smiled awkwardly. "Theirs," he

admitted, not able to look him in the eye.

"I had a hunch it was." Sid started out the door.

"Hey, Sid!" Ewing grabbed his sleeve. "Look, you saved me from alcohol a while back, remember? Now I'm sober and I'm going to stay that way. You've given me something to live for."

"I don't deserve all the thanks. Val helped out."

"Of course Val did," Gary said, nodding. "But don't you see what I'm saying? You won't go bankrupt."

Sid chuckled. "I'd like to believe that."

"You won't. If it's in my power, you're going to stay afloat in this business. Someway, somehow, we'll keep Knots Landing Motors on top—not just surviving, but on top!" Gary's eyes were alive with fire as he released the man's arm.

Selma Messinger ambled to her front door. "Who in hell could that be?" she grumbled. "You expecting one of your boyfriends, Pam?" she asked her daughter, who sat on the bed painting her toenails.

"No, not with you here." She blew a bright green bubble and popped it noisily.

Selma opened the front door. "What do you want?"

Karen Fairgate stood before her, dressed in a simple blue blouse, tight white jeans, her hair pulled back in a ponytail. "I just wanted to talk to you and Pam," Karen said. "Please?

For a minute anyway?" She looked at the woman hopefully.

"Well, all right." She opened the door and stepped back to let Karen in. "Pam, we've got company. The pervert's wife."

"Would you stop calling him that?" Karen asked patiently.

Pam stuffed the brush back into the bottle of "French Lavender" nail polish and waved her toes in the air to dry. "So?" she asked, leaning back on her elbows and enjoying her gum.

Karen sighed. "I just thought we might talk for a little while, maybe find a way to come to an understanding about this whole thing." Karen said the words carefully, trying to remain calm and collected.

"Then you might as well turn around and leave, lady," Selma said. "There's nothing to talk about."

"Yes, there is. There's my husband's life."

"Your husband, the child molester?" Pam asked.

Karen waited a moment before replying. "He didn't molest you or anyone else. And I'd hardly call you a child. Maybe if I told you about our family, the neighborhood we live in, and my relationship with Sid . . ."

"We don't want to hear all that," Selma said.

"You're going to." Karen's face hardened. "Just so you'll know what you're destroying with your daughter's stories."

"I'm not destroying you," Pam said

innocently, still waving her toes in the air. "It's your husband. He's the one who's ruined your life. He has to learn to keep his hands off young girls."

"Sid doesn't touch young girls. That's a lie and you know it!"

"Lady, I know your husband better than you ever could," Pam said evilly.

"You're lying! Admit it! Admit you made it all up because Sid wouldn't pay you money!"

Pam laughed.

"Go ahead, Pam! Now's your chance to clear yourself, before you're thrown in jail for perjury!"

"There's nothing to admit, Mrs. Fairgate!" Selma bellowed. "Because my daughter's telling the truth."

"Can't you understand what this is doing to my family? My daughter, Diana, is one year younger than Pam. Think how—"

"I can imagine this Diana," Pam said nastily. "A spoiled little rich girl, dressed in the best clothes, going to the best schools, with the right friends, perfect teeth, perfect—"

Karen shook her head. "You've got it all wrong, Pam. Diana sews most of the things she wears. She's not spoiled in the least. And she attends Knots Landing High—not a prep school. This is ruining her life."

"That doesn't change the fact that your husband tried to rape my daughter," Selma said, walking up to the woman. "We don't want to hear your sob stories, sister. So clear on out of here!"

"Can you honestly tell me that you believe Pam?" Karen asked in amazement.

Selma hesitated for a moment, glanced at Pam, then nodded. "Sure."

Karen stared at her, open-mouthed, then walked outside.

Selma Messinger rushed after her and stood on the porch.

"Mother!" Pam cried.

"Never mind, Pam. Stay here. I'll take care of this." She yelled out to Karen. "Hey, Mrs. Fairgate, your husband's a sick man. He needs help!" She followed Karen into the apartment complex's courtyard.

Karen stopped and turned to her. "Not more than ten seconds ago you looked at your daughter with doubt in your eyes. I could tell you were uncertain for a second—I saw it on your face. You know she's lying—oh, you may not want to admit it, but you *know!* But you hid those doubts."

"Sure, for a second I wondered. I always see the worst side of things, expect the worst. But that doesn't mean I think my daughter's lying. Mrs. Fairgate, I'm proud that she's standing up for her rights like this. It's telling me she thinks we're okay, the two of us, whatever else we may be. We're worth something. And lady, that takes courage."

"It takes a lot more than that," Karen said. "It takes a flair for lying."

"Now wait a minute!"

"Look, Mrs. Messinger, I'm all for what you're saying. I think everyone has their rights. I agree that there is a fundamental difference between deciding to do something and having something forced on you. I would be marching at Pam's side to the ends of the earth on this—*if* it weren't my husband she was accusing, and *if* she weren't lying. My husband is innocent; he certainly didn't try to rape your daughter."

"How can you be so sure?" Selma asked.

"I've known him for seventeen years. He's the gentlest, most loving man I've ever met. He simply isn't the kind of man who could do such a thing."

Selma smiled proudly. "Yeah? Well, what would you think of a man who told his lawyer to bribe Pam to drop the charges?"

Karen shook her head. "What are you talking about?"

"Lady, your husband's lawyer showed up here and offered my daughter a trip to Hawaii, a friend's condo, a surfboard, scuba gear, clothing—the whole nine yards."

"I don't believe it!"

"It didn't work. We turned him down, Pam and I." Selma smiled with satisfaction. "But does that sound like something an innocent man would do?"

"He did no such thing!" Karen shrieked.

"Hey, lady, I may fight dirty and kick when the other guy's down, but I never lie. The Messingers don't lie. That seems to be a Fairgate trait."

"You—"

"Go ahead. Ask that little slimy runt of a lawyer your husband hired."

Selma said the words with such conviction that Karen stopped for a moment and looked at her. "Believe me, I will," she said. "But I can't believe it's true."

"He tried to bribe Pam. He's guilty as anyone ever was."

"No!" Karen walked to her car, trying to forget the woman's awful words. As she started to pull away from the curb, a brightly painted orange van pulled up in front of her, then backed into the parking space.

As she shifted into reverse, Karen happened to see the van's license plate.

" 'I-C-K,' " she read, and frowned. "My feelings exactly—ick!"

A long-haired boy jumped down from the van as Karen backed out of the parking lot, still seething.

The boy disappeared into the apartment complex as Karen drove off. So many thoughts were running through her head. She knew Sid had no part in any bribery attempt—but Richard?

She had a few things to discuss with that man, she thought angrily.

Abby, Olivia, Brian and Val relaxed under the hot sun on Knots Landing Beach. Val was lying on her towel, watching the kids build a sand castle on the beach. They'd chosen a spot too close to the water, and the waves threatened to pull their fairy-tale structure down.

"How do you like Knots Landing?" Val asked Abby, as the two women studied Brian and Olivia's progress.

"It certainly is never dull here," Abby said. "I know Sid would be thrilled if I decided to stay longer, but the kids have to be back in school."

"That would be a problem, wouldn't it?" she said. "Do you have family in San Diego?"

Abby shot her a wary look. "No."

"Oh," Val said. "I guess I figured that was why you're moving there."

"No. I've been to San Diego, and I like it," she replied, a bit defensive. "La Jolla with its fabulous stores and restaurants; the miles of beaches; Mexico a few miles away." She sighed. "And those tanned gods walking up and down the streets."

"Oh," Val said, grinning. "Them!"

"Besides, now that Jeff and I have split for good, I figure I should do what I want to do. I felt that marrying Jeff was something I *had* to do."

"What about moving to Knots Landing?"

"I've never really liked Los Angeles," Abby said, watching the children run away from the waves. "But I'm having a pretty good time here—with the exception of Sid's case, of course."

"It might be nice for all of you. Olivia and Brian would be near their cousins, and you'd be near Sid."

"That's true."

"And think of the babysitting possibilities!" Val said. "If you wanted to spend some time alone, or go out on the town, you wouldn't have to worry about the children."

Abby raised an eyebrow and smiled. "I'll certainly think about it, Val," she said, and lay down on her towel to soak up some more sun.

"Great!" Val said, continuing to watch the boy and girl at the edge of the sea, her eyes shining.

Abby smiled to herself, staring up at the brilliantly blue California sky. With all the attractions of Knots Landing—including the handsome men living on Seaview Circle— she just might be persuaded to move there.

Karen sat alone in the middle of her living room. The shades were drawn, the lights off, the house silent as a tomb. She had cried herself out long ago. All she could do now was sit and worry.

How could he? The question echoed in her mind as she sat in the darkness. How could Richard have tried to bribe Pam Messinger into dropping the charges against Sid?

It was unbelievable. No wonder Richard had been so secretive.

The garage door banged open and Sid walked into the kitchen. "Honey?" he called, flicking on lights as he walked into the living room.

"Hi, Sid," Karen said morosely.

"What are you doing? Everything okay?"

"No. When I got home, I went through the house shutting the drapes upstairs and down. I don't know why . . . or maybe I do."

Sid sat down beside her.

"I didn't expect you back so early," she said quietly.

"Well, there's not much to do at work." Sid studied his wife curiously. "Besides, Gary can handle everything."

Looking at her husband, Karen was surprised to see how much Sid had aged in the last few days. He looked so tired. "Sid, I hate to say this, but we're finished. Doomed. We might as well give up."

"What are you talking about? Why are we finished?"

"Your trial, Sid. You've lost."

"Hey, what's gotten into you? Where'd you go this afternoon?"

"I went to Pam Messinger's apartment."

His mouth opened in amazement. "You're kidding."

Karen shook her head. "I thought I could talk some sense into them. Instead, they told me something awful. Sid, Richard tried to bribe Pam."

"What?" He gasped.

"He offered her a trip to Hawaii, some nice clothes, time in a condo—I don't know what else. But it didn't work. They turned him down. And when this gets out in court . . ." Karen shivered, and buried her face in her husband's shoulder.

An hour later, Sid Fairgate looked out his front window. Richard Avery and his son, Jason, had just pulled up in their driveway. Frowning, Sid steeled himself. Karen had already called Stan Loesser. Now he had one last thing to do.

Sid left his house and walked out to the Avery's driveway.

"Hi, Sid!" Richard said, getting out of his car. "You look awful," he said, crossing to his mailbox. Seven-year-old Jason tagged along at his feet like a puppy, grinning up at his daddy.

"Richard, is it true?" Sid asked solemnly.

Avery looked at him. "Yes, it's true—you look awful."

"No. Karen told me that you tried to bribe Pam Messinger."

The man stepped back in surprise. "Where'd she hear that?" he asked, his face suddenly pale.

"Is it true?"

"No. Well, yes, I guess, technically."

"What?" Sid asked, astonished.

"I thought I could talk her out of—"

"Richard, you're fired. I hired Stan Loesser to represent me in this trial."

Richard broke into a sweat. "What? You're joking, Sid, right?"

"I can't let you jeopardize my future any longer. You may already have ruined my chances for an acquittal, but maybe I can still pull through." He started to turn away.

"Hey! Wait a minute!" Richard said,

frowning. "Why am I suddenly the bad guy? I did this for *you!*"

"I wouldn't be in this mess if I'd just given Pam the hundred dollars she asked for. Don't you see? Your bribe makes you as bad as Pam."

"Yeah, but paying her's the only chance you'll have of clearing this thing up, Sid."

"I'm innocent, and they don't send innocent men to jail."

Richard laughed scornfully. "Will you grow up, Sid? You're not that stupid. This is reality. This is your life. Things don't always work out the way they should. Why not ease your morality a bit?"

"I don't need any more advice from you, Richard. As of now, you no longer represent me!" Sid's face was flushed with emotion as he turned and walked back to his house.

Richard stood frozen at the foot of his driveway. Jason reached into the mailbox and pulled out a few letters, then handed them to his father.

But Richard did not notice the boy. He was staring at the Fairgates' house, his face pale with fear and desperation.

Laura carefully inserted the endless roll of address labels into her typewriter, lined up the first one, and glanced at her copy. Another mailing list to do this afternoon. She looked at her watch. She'd never be home by five. Another late work day.

Her phone rang. Laura picked up the

receiver. "Warren-Southland Realty," she said briskly.

"Laura?"

"Richard?" Laura let the list drop to her desk. "Hi. What's up?" she said coolly.

Her husband hesitated at the other end. "I don't know."

"Richard, I'm busy right now. What's on your mind?"

"He . . . he . . ."

Laura sighed, her frown deepening. "Have you been drinking again, Richard?" She could practically smell the booze over the wire.

"Laura!"

She shook her head, looking at the watch, her typewriter, and the list of addresses. She couldn't take another interruption. "Look, honey, I've got a ton of work to do by five. I'll probably be late as it is. I'll talk to you later, okay?"

"Laura!" Richard cried frantically.

Frowning, she gently set the phone down on its cradle and began typing.

Chapter Eight

New Hope

"It must have been hard on him," Stan Loesser said to Karen and Sid as they sat in his study that afternoon. "But you did the right thing."

"Is the case doomed?" Karen asked, her voice trembling. "I mean, what will happen when the jury finds out what Richard tried to do? Are clients responsible for their lawyer's actions?"

"I don't know," Stan said. "We'll have to see. But in the meantime, with all the material we have to go through, maybe I can find some small points in your favor."

Sid was interested. "Points?"

"Yeah, maybe Pam slipped up somewhere. Maybe she hasn't always told the same story."

"Maybe," Karen said doubtfully.

Stan looked over the papers on his desk, interested in Pam's statement. Then he pulled out the newspaper article and scanned it quickly. He tapped the paper. "Hmm. I thought so!"

"Thought what?" Sid asked.

"Sid, the girl said you offered to pay her one hundred dollars to have sex with you. That's in her official statement as well as the two newspaper articles. Do you still have the receipt the police gave you when they took your personal belongings?"

"No. The only way I could get my stuff back was to hand over the receipt."

"No problem. I'll have a copy made. Now, this is important. How much cash did you have with you that night? Do you remember the amount on the receipt?"

Sid shook his head.

"Okay. A hundred dollars?" the lawyer asked.

"No. Too high."

Stan smiled. "How much less? Ninety?"

"I'd say around eighty or so."

"Good. That's an example of the Messinger girl's statements being inconsistent with the facts. We can prove how much money you had that night with the police receipt."

"In other words?" Karen asked.

"How could Sid Fairgate say he'd give that girl a hundred dollars? He didn't have it."

"That's right!" Sid said.

"But there's no proof that he ever meant to pay her, so he could have been lying about how much money he had. That's what they'll use," Karen said, alarmed.

"Probably," the handsome lawyer agreed. "But if I can find enough inconsistencies, it won't be so easy to explain them away." He warmed to the subject. "I can call in character witnesses to testify that Sid's life is perfectly respectable. Even if the jury believes that his one flaw is a secret desire for young girls, all the conflicting evidence we bring in will shake their conviction."

"Well, maybe," Sid said.

Stan smiled. "Oh, sure, it's a gamble. Everything's a gamble in court."

"Great! I always lose at poker."

"I know there's more here, buried in this paperwork, and I'll spend the rest of the day and night looking for it. I know we can clear you of all charges, Sid. I don't think Avery's idea of plea bargaining was a good one."

"It's a relief to hear you say that," Karen admitted.

"Stan, thanks for your help," Sid said. "Sorry I didn't call you sooner."

"No problem. And if either of you think of anything that doesn't seem right in Pam's story, let me know. I don't care if it's five in the morning—call me. Okay?"

"We will. Thanks, Stan," Karen said. "I'll try not to worry any more. Maybe I'll take up yoga or something to get my mind off this."

"You do that. See you tomorrow if not before."

The Fairgates walked out of the lawyer's expensive home. They gazed out at the sea and the beautiful beach property on which the house was built.

"You know, Karen, Stan Loesser must be pretty good to live in a home like this."

"Laura told me Scooter sold him this place. You want to know the price?"

"I'm not sure I do," Sid said as they walked to their car.

"One and a half million."

Sid whistled as he unlocked Karen's door. "I guess we don't have anything to worry about."

Karen got in the car and smiled.

Richard took a healthy swallow of whiskey before pouring it over the sizzling steaks in the skillet. The pan exploded into flames, charring the meat and singeing Richard's hair.

"Hey!" he said, dancing back drunkenly. He stared at the five-inch high flames that were busily burning off the liquor and charring the expensive meat.

"Should have broiled the steaks, I guess," Richard mumbled. "What the hell. I'll burn 'em—like Sid burned me." He tipped the bottle over the pan, and flames leaped into the air.

His kitchen filled with smoke as the lawyer drank deeply from the bottle. The more he drank, Richard thought dully, the more he could forget about Sid Fairgate and how the man had dumped him.

He never even gave me a chance, Richard

thought, watching the flames like an ancient priest studying a bonfire for glimpses of the future. None came.

"I should put that fire out," Richard said out loud, then laughed. He stumbled back as the fire brightened, reached its zenith and began dying down. The pan and its contents were charred and blackened.

Angry that the show had ended, Richard dashed more liquor into the pan.

"What is going on here!" Laura Avery cried, stumbling past her husband. She grabbed a box of baking soda from the cabinet and threw the white powder at the base of the flames, smothering them. Laura turned back to her husband.

He grinned at her, unsteady on his feet. He was holding the whiskey bottle. "Hi, honey. Dinner's almost . . . ready."

"You nearly burned the whole house down, Richard," Laura told him, opening the windows.

"Cut it out!" he said, suddenly angry. "I'm having fun. I always thought women's things like cooking were supposed to be hard work. But it's not."

"Not the way you do it. Why are you drinking?" Laura frowned. "From your appearance, I'd say you must have started hours ago."

Richard narrowed his bloodshot eyes. "Why not? Breathe California air and you get drunk."

Laura picked up a pot holder and took the

pan to the sink, where she dumped out the shriveled remains of the steaks.

"Honey, don't be a party pooper. I'm celebrating," Richard said, clutching the bottle protectively. It was nearly empty.

"What could you possibly have to celebrate?" Laura demanded.

"Your new career, Sid's future in-car-cer-a-tion," Richard said slowly, concentrating on each syllable, "and my firing."

"What?"

Richard's eyes rolled. "Ask Fairgate, that traitor, that paragon of virtue who lives next door. You know, he never really liked me. He just pretended to like me."

"Richard, why don't you just—"

"Sid gave me my walking papers today. He canned me, told me to take a hike, twisted the knife as he pulled it out from my back, waited until I wasn't looking to kick my legs out from under me . . ." He looked up at her. "You want me to go on?"

"Sid fired you?"

"Yeah. I guess he has this Joan of Arc complex. He wants to be a martyr."

"Why?" Laura asked. "He must have a good reason."

Richard saw his wife eyeing him dubiously. "There wasn't any reason."

"Come on, Richard. What did you do to Sid?"

"Hey, don't ask me that. Ask what Sid did to me! He—he—"

"He took you off the case," Laura said.

"But I'm sure he had a good reason."

"Hey, I'm not gonna stand for this," he said, and started unsteadily for the door.

"Where are you going, Richard?" Laura asked, running after him.

The lawyer rushed out into the night, staggering over to the Fairgates' lawn. "Hey, Sid, come on out here! I'm ready to knock you down. Let's have a little man-to-man fight!" He balled his fists. "Come on, backstabber! Get what's coming to you!"

"Richard, shut up and come home!" Laura pleaded from behind him, shivering in the cool night air.

"Shut up, Laura!" he yelled.

Sid appeared at his door, with Karen and Diana standing behind him. "What's up, Richard?" he asked.

"Come on, Fairgate! I'll fight you in your own lair." He swayed drunkenly. "Come on out here and put 'em up!"

"Go home, Richard. Call me in the morning."

"This *is* home," he said. "I'm your neighbor, remember? A neighbor's someone you trust your lawn mower with, or your wife—"

"Richard!" Laura shouted.

"Hey, Fairgate, I thought you were my friend. I'm the one who got you out of the slammer, remember? You called *me* at two in the morning to come get you."

Gary and Val Ewing walked up, roused by the loud voices.

"That's just the liquor in you talking," Gary said to Richard.

The man turned toward him shakily. "Jealous?" he asked savagely. "I'll bet you're just dying for a drink. Straight up, on the rocks, with a twist? Shooters, doubles, sidecars?"

"That's enough, Richard!" Sid said, hurrying down the steps.

"I've seen you sneaking drinks on your way home from those 'recovering alcoholics' sessions at the hospital." Richard leered.

"Hey, Richard," Gary said, still cool. "Come on. Go back home and sleep it off." Val had her arm around her husband's waist, holding on for comfort.

"I'll handle this, Gary," Sid said, and walked up to Richard. "He's my monster. I created him. But I never thought he'd act like this."

"Well, you thought wrong, didn't you, Mr. Morality!" Richard smiled smugly.

Sid frowned in the dim streetlight. "You may have cost me my future."

The man giggled. "I don't see anything wrong with that. You know how rape cases go. Everyone loses. Pam's gotta know that. It doesn't matter if you're innocent or not. No one cares!"

"I care!" Sid said furiously. "You ruined my chances for a good defense!"

"This is the thanks I get for trying to save your hide?" Richard said. "You can't see it, can you? You lost the second you let that girl into your car." He stumbled slightly.

"For pete's sake, I was helping out a girl in trouble!" Sid cried.

Richard laughed. "Yeah. I'm sure every jury in the country would believe you, Sid. Come off your high horse. She's a cute, tempting little thing. She's no angel, but that doesn't matter."

"That's enough," Laura said.

"Yeah, they'll think you picked her up because she's young, beautiful, and has an incredible—"

Sid grabbed Richard's shirt front and twisted it firmly. He held the man for a second. "Listen to me!"

"No." Richard broke free from Sid's hand, and fell to the moist grass as he lost his balance. "You're guilty, Sid! Face it! You better get used to hearing the word. Guilty! Guilty! You'll be locked up by the end of the week!"

"Come on home, Sid," Karen said.

Sid glanced at her, then nodded.

Gary and Val slipped quietly away as Laura stood over her husband, shaking her head.

"You really did it this time, didn't you, Richard? Happy?"

He smiled as he looked up at his wife, flat on his back.

"Oh, Richard!" Laura said.

He writhed on the grass, his face twisted with anger as he was unable to pull himself up. "Help me!" he said irritably.

Laura's cheeks shone as silent tears

slipped down them. "Help yourself," she murmured, and walked away in disgust.

Abby's hips swung gently as she walked into the showroom of Knots Landing Motors. She was wearing a white silk blouse open halfway to her navel, tight blue jeans, and black high heels. She looked very chic, and she knew it.

She walked to Gary's office, and found it empty.

"I hate it," a familiar voice said behind her.

Abby turned and saw Gary Ewing holding a proposed display ad for the dealership.

"Hope I'm not interrupting anything," she said, smiling sweetly as she walked up to Gary.

"We'll talk about this later," he said to Jim, the dealership's ad man.

"I tried," Jim said and walked away, leaving Gary holding the layout.

"Hello, Abby. No, you're not interrupting me. I just don't like this ad." He held it out to her. "What do you think? Might as well get a woman's opinion."

Abby wrinkled her nose. "I don't know. It's pushy, Gary," she said bluntly.

"Don't I know it! It's hard selling cars— inflation and the energy crisis aren't exactly great incentives for people to buy cars."

"That makes sense," Abby said. "Gary, is Sid around? I didn't see him out there."

"Probably in his office." He moved closer to her. "People haven't been treating him well—even his own employees."

"You mean because of the rape trial?" she asked incredulously. "He should fire them. All of them. They've got no right to treat Sid like that!"

"Abby, it's a natural reaction."

"I don't care. Natural or not, my brother doesn't have to take that kind of treatment from his own employees!"

"Look, Abby, Sid's just keeping himself busy with paperwork and reading the trades. Sort of, you know—"

"Hiding out?"

"Well, I wouldn't call it that exactly. There's a nicer way of saying it."

"Believe me, Gary, there's no reason to be nice with me. I'm Sid's sister, after all."

He sighed again. "Sorry, Abby. It's just the business. It's got me thinking crazy."

She looked around the empty showroom. "Things do look bad."

"We'll scrape by if the courts vindicate Sid. Then it'll be business as usual. I'm hoping a turn around in the economy and a sudden oversupply of oil show up soon, too."

Abby smiled at the handsome man. "I know I can trust Sid's well-being with you. You'll pull him through this."

Gary smiled shyly, then shrugged. "Where're the kids?"

"Val's watching them for me. They really seem to have taken a liking to her." She continued to gaze at him, fully aware of her striking beauty.

"I noticed. Val's told me all about it, and she couldn't be happier."

"Great," Abby said, eyes shining. "It must be this Southern California air." She held his gaze until the man looked away.

"What about the air?" he asked, glancing back to her.

"It seems love's in the air. Everyone's feeling it," she said, and ran her tongue over her lips.

"But nothing's real here. Oh, some things are, but not what you think. Walk behind it and you'll see the supports holding up the flats. Look up and you'll see the lights."

"But illusion can become reality with the right ingredients. Don't you agree?" Abby practically purred at him.

"Maybe. Once in a while."

She smiled.

"Hey, buddy, what are you trying to do to me? Yeah, you'll pay for it—every last cent!" Sid's voice boomed from the cashier's desk.

Abby frowned, upset that the moment had ended. She looked at Sid and hurried over to him, aware that Gary had followed.

Sid stood before an irate, red-faced man with a beer gut and short, greasy hair. He clutched a repair bill in his hand.

"No way, Fairgate!" the man snapped.

"It's the law. We reconnected your smog device because it wasn't hooked up. We have to charge for work like that."

"I never *asked* you—" the man began, stabbing the bill with his index finger.

"You didn't have to!" Sid shouted, his face reddening. "It's the law! And besides, I'm sick of air pollution! Anything I can do to keep from breathing your car fumes, I'll do! So pay the nice lady before I call the cops," Sid warned. He saw Abby. "Hey! Can you believe that? The guy thinks he doesn't have to pay because we rehooked his catalytic converter without asking him. I couldn't pass inspection on that car without doing it. That's what we have laws for! And in the end, it protects us, because it protects the air!"

"Right," Abby said.

"I don't know," Sid said and disappeared into his office.

Abby and Gary stopped just outside the doorway after exchanging a worried look. Sid stood before his desk, fuming. Suddenly he swept his arm across it, flinging pictures, pens, brochures, papers, and a vase with a dying rose onto the floor.

Abby stepped back, pressing against Gary, as the glass vase shattered.

"That's what the law is for, right?" Sid asked, then slammed the door shut.

Abby and Gary stared at the closed door in shock, then turned to each other. Abby bit her lower lip. Gary just shook his head and didn't say a word.

Richard walked down the hallway toward Warren William Simpson's office. He felt nervous, edgy. He was still groggy from the previous night, during which, he remembered vaguely, he'd burned his dinner, consumed most of a bottle of whiskey, and terrorized his neighborhood. Not bad for a slow evening at home.

The outer office was again empty, so Richard tapped on Simpson's door.

"Come in."

Richard pushed it open and entered the office. Mr. Simpson sat reading a newspaper at his desk.

"Mr. Avery," he said by way of greeting. He then let the paper fall, revealing a photograph of Pam Messinger flashing a victory sign at the camera. Above it the headline read: "Teen Vows to Send Attempted Rapist to Jail."

"I saw the article," Richard said.

"Yes. She sure has been keeping busy, courting the press this way."

"It would seem so, sir," Richard said.

"Mr. Avery, I've decided that Don Hanover will be joining you on this case—as a criminal law consultant, you understand." The lawyer fell silent for a moment. "He'll assist you in preparing your case, and will be there in court with you if you need him."

Richard looked at his boss glumly.

"This is in no way a criticism of your talents, Avery. But as you represent Pincus, Simpson and Lyle, and this case is gaining a bit of notoriety, we want to be sure you use every resource available to you. And Don Hanover's the expert in criminal cases. What do you think about that?" he asked lightly.

You don't care what I think, Richard wanted to say, but he held back the words. "I'm sorry, Mr. Simpson, but I'm off the Fairgate case."

"I beg your pardon?"

"I won't be representing Sid Fairgate."

"Why not?"

"We had a difference of opinion in how his defense should be handled." He frowned. "We're also neighbors and friends, and he let it get in the way of our lawyer-client relationship. I value my friendship with Fairgate far too much to allow anything to jeopardize it," Avery said slowly, in his best courtroom voice.

"Has Mr. Fairgate met Don Hanover?"

"Not to my knowledge," Richard answered. "He's using Stan Loesser now."

"Loesser?" Simpson nodded. "Good man. He won that noteworthy Evans case last year." He looked at his paper again, clearly finished with Richard. "I respect your decision."

"Thank you, sir. Good day." Richard turned to the door.

"Indeed."

As he walked out of the office, Richard was sure he felt the old man peering over the edge of his newspaper at him. He hoped he'd fooled the old guy.

Olivia sat patiently in the chair while Val stood over her, brushing her long black hair until it shone in the light. Nearby, Brian was bent over a coloring book, working furiously.

"And the tree is blue, and the sky is red, and the sun is purple," the boy said.

"Brian, you don't even know how to color," his sister teased.

"I do too! I just want to color this way."

"He's creative," Val said, smiling.

"Should I cut my bangs?" the girl asked her.

"I think that should be your mother's decision."

Olivia shrugged. "She'll say she likes it no matter how I do it."

Val frowned. "But you might as well ask her before you do anything too drastic, okay, Olivia?"

She smiled. "Okay."

"See?" Brian said, holding up his picture for Val to see.

Val looked at it, a perfectly normal scene of blue sky, green grass, and a shimmering yellow-orange sun. "That's wonderful," Val said.

"I thought—" Olivia started, then smiled as she looked at the picture. "That's good, Brian."

"Thanks."

The door burst open and Abby ran in, laden with bags and boxes. She had been out shopping. Abby set her load on the couch. "Sorry I'm late, Val. Hi, kids."

"Late?" the Southern woman asked. "I've been having such a good time, I didn't even notice." She set the brush on a table.

"Look, Mommy!" Brian said, thrusting the picture up into his mother's face.

"Mommy, I want to cut my bangs," Olivia said. "Can I?"

"See my picture? I can color!"

"Yes, fine, that's nice, Brian," Abby said, and turned to her daughter. Both children began talking at once. "Hold it!" Abby said. "I can't hear a word you're saying! One at a time, okay?"

"But I was talking first!" Brian said.

"But this is important!" Olivia wailed.

"Children! Enough!"

Val sat back, shaking her head. Everything had been fine until Val came home.

"I'm sorry," Abby said, flustered. "You've got to learn how to take turns *talking*, along with everything else."

Olivia suddenly grabbed the coloring book from Brian's hand. He started to wail and spilled his crayons on the carpet.

"That's *mine*, Olivia!"

"That's *mine*, Olivia!" his sister screamed in almost perfect imitation.

"Oh brother, not again!" Abby said.

"Oh brother, not again!"

"Olivia!" Brian yelled, reaching for his book.

"Olivia!" she said, and ran from the room.

Brian trailed after her. "Mommy!"

"Mommy!"

Abby shook her head, exasperated. "How can you keep up with them?" she said. "I've been here less than a minute and I'm already exhausted."

"Oh, we have fun," Val said, her eyes shining. "They really are wonderful children."

"Olivia, it's mine!" Brian's muffled voice called out.

"Olivia, it's mine!"

Abby smiled. "They sure are."

Chapter Nine

Memory Loss

Karen sat in the back seat of Stan Loesser's Cadillac as they drove to the scene of the supposed crime. Sid sat in front beside the lawyer.

"I wonder if this will ever be forgotten, so we can get back to our normal lives," Karen said. "How long will it go on?"

Stan smiled. "That depends mostly on the outcome of the trial."

"Go on," Sid said, as he relived the events of the awful night.

"If Sid's convicted, your harassment may never end." He parked the car in the area where the crime had occurred, leaving the lights on to brighten the street.

"Great!" Karen groaned.

"If the case ends with a hung jury and is dismissed, things'll be better, but there'll always be the suspicion of your guilt, Sid."

"So what's left?"

"An acquittal, for one thing. But even then it may not be over." He glanced at Sid.

"Why not?" Karen asked, exasperated.

"If Sid's acquitted that doesn't mean he hasn't been tried and convicted in the public mind. Folks are smart today. They know not all trials end fairly. Some may think the state simply didn't do its job of proving that Sid's guilty."

"So this lie will be with us for the rest of our lives?" Karen asked tensely.

"Perhaps," Stan said. "But there are a couple of alternatives, though neither seems likely. Pam Messinger might confess that the story isn't true. That would let Sid off the hook for good. Or the D.A. might dismiss the case."

"Would he?" Karen asked, turning to Sid, who continued to stare out the window.

"Sure, if there's just cause. For instance, if it could be proven that she's lying."

"Is that your plan?" Karen asked.

"Well, that would be great, but I'm not counting on it. There's no hard evidence—it's her story against Sid's. It'll be tough . . . but let's get to work." He opened his car door.

The street seemed dark and lonely as the three stepped from the car and stood on the grimy sidewalk. Karen clutched her purse and glanced around the area. It was an industrial part of town and seemed devoid of life.

"Okay," Stan said, turning to Sid. "What happened on your way to Knots Landing

High School that night? Tell me again."

He sighed. "I was stopped at a red light. A young girl stuck her head into my car and asked me for a ride. I told her I was in a hurry and, although it was hard to do, turned her down. I drove through the intersection and saw this guy from a van jump out toward her and grab her. Naturally, I backed up and let her in."

"What happened after that?" Stan asked.

"I drove off, as fast as I could."

"And the van?"

"I guess it pulled away from the curb."

"You're not sure?" Stan asked.

"Wait, it followed us. Yeah, it was pretty close behind us for a while, but then it just sort of disappeared."

"How long did the van follow you?" Stan asked.

Sid shook his head. "I couldn't tell you." Then suddenly, he brightened.

"What is it?" Karen asked.

"I just remembered something, but it doesn't seem possible."

"I'll be the judge of that," Loesser said.

"When the police were arresting me, the van drove by."

"It did?" Stan asked, looking at the man intently. "You never mentioned that before."

"I know, I know. I just remembered."

Stan walked to the car and grabbed a document from it, then held it under the headlight's glare to read.

"Is the van important?" Karen asked

thoughtfully, crossing her arms.

"Maybe. Pam's statement says Sid just stopped by the side of the road as she was walking and asked her if she wanted a ride. There's nothing here about that van."

"But she mentioned it at least once," Karen said.

"When?"

"It was that night that Richard and I went to pick up Sid at the station. She was yelling at us, screaming, because Sid was being released. She said—"

"I remember!" Sid exclaimed.

"She said Sid had tried to scare her by telling her things like, 'Guess what the guys in the van are gonna do to you?'"

"Really?" Stan asked. "So the girl made her statement but didn't say a word about the van. Then not long after, she yelled at you, and mentions the van. Then during the preliminary hearing, she again withheld your supposed threat to her involving this van."

"I see," Karen said. "When she's herself, relaxed, she tells the police what she wants to tell them. But when she's angry, like she was that night, she loses control and says whatever comes into her head."

"She's intentionally lying," Sid said.

"Exactly. But why?"

Karen frowned. "Maybe she knew the men in the van."

"Bingo! It's pretty simple. She must have some kind of scam operation going on with the men who were 'hassling' her on the street. That's why she didn't mention them to the police." Stan turned to Sid. "Think, Sid. Think hard."

"I'll try." He furrowed his brow in concentration.

"Remember that night. Recall exactly what happened. What did the van look like? What make was it? What color?"

Sid closed his eyes and struggled for a moment. Then he shook his head. "I'm sorry. I don't have the slightest idea."

"Keep trying," Stan said. "I think we've done all we can here. Let's go home."

As they stepped into the car, Sid frowned. "My mind's a complete blank. But I saw the van for at least a minute."

"You'll remember, Sid. You've got to," Karen pleaded.

An hour later, Karen sat in her kitchen, sipping coffee with Abby.

"How'd you get your kids to be so quiet?" Karen asked. "I haven't heard a peep out of them in two days. What are you doing, drugging them?"

"Val," Abby said, stirring her coffee.

"Val's drugging them?"

Abby smiled. "No. She's watching them. That woman pleaded with me to let her take them for the night."

Karen smiled at her skeptically. "Really?"

Sid walked in, took a glass from the cupboard, and went to the refrigerator.

"Hi, honey," Karen said. "Still thinking?"

"Yeah." He poured himself a glass of milk.

"Any luck yet?" Abby asked, wiping her lips delicately with her napkin.

"Some. I've gone over every detail in my mind. Some of it's pretty hazy, but most of it's crystal clear." He took a swallow of milk. "I can see the van—in a three-quarter view from the front. I can even see the license plate—I can tell you exactly where it was on the van. But that's all. No numbers."

"Obviously you didn't think to look," Abby said. "Who would?"

"But I can remember the names on the street signs and I wasn't aware of looking at them." He slumped in the chair. "All I have to do is remember a couple of numbers and I may save myself. If I don't, everything I've worked for is gone." He rubbed his face with his hands. "There's too much at stake here."

Abby touched his arm. "Thing's will look up."

"Just relax, honey. Don't try to force it. Maybe if you lie down for a while you'll be able to think clearer." Karen took his empty milk glass from the table and put it in the sink.

"You could be right," Sid said. "I've got the worst headache I've ever had."

"Yeah, Sid, relax!" Abby said. "Things are always better if you let them come naturally."

"Thanks, both of you," Sid said, and went upstairs to his bedroom.

"Who would have thought something like

this would happen to us?" Karen mused as she rinsed out the glass at the sink.

"Karen, what can we do to help Sid?" Abby asked.

She shut off the water and turned toward her. This woman—at times her opponent, at times her friend—was opening up to Karen, offering her support. Abby's face wasn't as poised and confident as it usually was. Karen thought she saw Abby's true feelings surfacing.

"All we can do is trust Sid," she said. "He's never let us down before, and he won't let himself down now. He'll remember," she said with finality, and grabbed the dishtowel.

"But how can you know that?" Abby asked anxiously.

"I just do." Karen wiped the glass and set it in the cupboard. "You know, Abby, I never realized how much we had in common."

The other woman stepped back in surprise. "What are you talking about?" Her mask slipped back into place. She was suddenly suspicious, untrusting.

Karen blinked back the tears that suddenly sprang to her eyes. "We've both got Sid," she said, and returned to her seat at the table.

Abby walked over to her slowly. She started to lay a reassuring hand on Karen's shoulder, then withdrew it and sat opposite her sister-in-law.

"Let's hope for the best," Abby said. "It's all up to him, now."

* * *

That same night, Laura Avery left her books, figures and calculator in the study and went to her bedroom.

Richard sat in the center of the bed, smiling viciously, his ever-present bottle in hand.

"Are you going to drink in your sleep, too, Richard?" she asked, smelling alcohol in the air.

"Why? You want me to bring enough for you, too, sweetheart?" Richard made a wild gesture with his hand. "Why is it that you have to *question* me about *every* little thing I do? I mean, what's with you, lady? You're acting more like my mother than my wife."

"Shut up, Richard," Laura said. "You'll wake Jason." She watched her husband as he lay sulking in bed.

Richard sighed. "Don't say it, Laura. I can see it in your eyes."

"You're turning into an alcoholic."

He laughed. "One point for the little lady for observation! Hey, honey, thanks for the support."

"I mean it! You're drunk all the time, except when you're at work. That sounds serious to me. Don't you even care, Richard?"

He smiled lasciviously. "Come over here, woman, and I'll show you I care!"

Laura backed into the bathroom and shut the door behind her. She turned on the shower, trying to block out her husband's rantings which were clearly audible through the thin door.

After a brief shower, Laura dried herself and stepped back into her robe. *I should probably feel some pity for him,* Laura thought coldly, *but I don't. Richard got himself into this mess. He brought it on himself. Ever since he started stagnating at Pincus, Simpson and Lyle, he's been on a downhill streak. I should have seen it earlier, but until Richard's bribery attempt I thought my marriage had been the only thing falling apart.*

When Laura left the misty bathroom she found the bedroom empty. Richard was gone. She pulled back the covers, determined not to worry. But then she heard the car start outside. Where was he off to? Laura wondered. Perhaps there was another woman somewhere, one who would give him more sympathy and compassion than his wife? Perhaps he was going to see her now.

Laura slid between the cool sheets and reached over to turn off the bedroom light. But she could not sleep.

Where *was* he going? She kept asking herself. And perhaps more importantly, would he get there safely, as drunk as he was?

Gary and Val lay snuggled together in bed. Gary wrapped his arm around Val's shoulders, while his other hand stroked her blond hair.

"Incredible," he whispered.

"What's incredible?"

"You." He kissed her cheek.

"Gary, that tickles!" Val laughed and squirmed away from his eager lips.

He nuzzled her neck. Then he lifted his head and lay it back on the pillow with a sigh.

"Something wrong?" Val asked tenderly. She touched her husband's bare chest.

"I was just thinking about Sid. He's not getting a fair deal on this thing."

"I'll say. You should hear the gossip in town—everyone's talking about the case."

"I know it. You should see work. It's deserted most of the time." He frowned. "But what I hate most is what it's doing to Sid."

"Really? He seems fine."

"Yeah, around home he's okay. But he blew up at a customer at work. I've never seen him like that before, Val."

"Sid's been through a lot, Gary. But we know he's innocent. Right?" She pulled him closer to her for comfort.

"Of course."

She smiled sadly. "I just wish the rest of Knots Landing would believe that."

"There's been too much bad press. Maybe Richard was right," he said, sighing.

"Right about what?" she asked, her eyes guarded.

"No one wins in a rape trial. It pulls everyone down."

"I *can't* believe that and I *won't* believe that, Gary! Sid's going to come through this smelling like a rose. I believe that, and you've got to believe it, too, Gary, or you're not really his friend! Don't you see?"

He looked at her. "I want Sid to be acquitted as much as you, but I don't see how it's possible now."

"Stan Loesser will find a way," Val said. "He's one of the most successful lawyers around."

"Yeah, I know. I read the papers, too. I hope you're right, honey, but it's hard not to be cynical right now."

"That's when you need to look at the bright side the most." She kissed his cheek, his ear, and finally his mouth.

"Okay, honey," he murmured as their lips parted. "I'll put all my energy into thinking Sid will come out of this just fine."

"Good!" she said, snuggling closer against him. "Now, how about thinking about some . . . other things?"

Gary smiled and bit her ear.

Karen lay quietly in bed. She stared at the ceiling, then closed her eyes.

Beside her, her husband tossed and turned, too tortured by thoughts and fears to find sleep.

After an endless hour of sleeplessness, Karen finally turned to her husband.

"Sid?" she whispered.

"You're awake?"

"Tell me what the van looked like."

"Sure. It was just a van," Sid mumbled, exhaustion evident in his voice. "It was orange and red, with these flames on the front and sides . . ." His voice trailed off.

Sid was doing it, Karen thought. He was describing the van! Maybe he'd remember the license number.

" . . . and this wide strip down the center. It really stood out under the street lamps. Big tires, a license plate holder with the words HONK IF YOU'RE FEMALE."

Sid fell silent.

"I know that van," Karen said slowly, realization dawning on her. "I saw it just the other day."

Sid bolted up from the bed, fully awake. "You're kidding!"

"No, I'm not." Karen felt breathless with excitement.

"Where did you see it?"

"I saw it pull up outside Pam Messinger's house as I was leaving. In fact, it parked directly in front of me."

"That's incredible! Do you know what this means? Somehow, Pam is familiar with those guys in the van!"

"There's more," Karen said, her voice trembling. "I remember part of the license number."

"Seriously?" Sid asked guardedly. "How?"

"I happened to notice it and I laughed. I had just stormed out of that place, after failing miserably to talk them out of pressing charges. I was so angry and upset and sick inside that I couldn't wait to get back home." Karen swallowed. "Then the van showed up and when I saw the license I thought it fit my feelings perfectly."

"I'm not following you, Karen," Sid said, shaking his head.

"The letters on the license plate, Sid. They were I-C-K. 'Ick.' It summed up my feelings toward the Messingers perfectly."

Sid stared at her in wonder, broke into a huge grin, and tackled her on the bed.

"Sid!" Karen laughed, falling back against the pillows.

"I love you, do you know that, Karen?"

"I love you, too."

They kissed.

"What do we do now?" Sid asked.

Karen reached for the phone. "Stan Loesser told us to call him if you thought of anything that might help. I know it's late, Sid . . . but something tells me this is worth waking him up for . . ."

Sid smiled at her, hope written all over his face. "You know, sweetheart, thanks to you my luck has suddenly changed!"

Chapter Ten

The Pieces Come Together

Laura glanced out her window. Thomas Burkhead, one of Warren-Southland Realty's top salesmen, was leaving the vacant house that sat beside the Averys' on Seaview Circle. He was followed by a young couple.

She dashed out of the house, then slowed to a walk as she neared the trio. Thomas saw her and waved. As the couple went to the car, the salesman met Laura.

"What did they think?" she asked breathlessly.

"Thanks for telling me about the house. It's great," Burkhead said. "But they aren't taking it."

Laura's face fell. "Why not?"

"The location. You never told me you lived next door to Sid Fairgate."

"I . . . it never came up, I guess. Why does it make a difference?"

The salesman's smile was ironic. "They

163

spent the whole trip here telling me how much they want a nice neighborhood for their fifteen-year-old daughter to live in." He shook his head. "When they saw the Fairgate's mailbox at the foot of the drive, they quickly changed their minds about this place. But they were nice enough to look at the house."

Laura closed her eyes. "I'm sorry."

"No problem," Thomas said. "But I'm afraid that house'll be empty for a long time. At least until Sid Fairgate moves out of the neighborhood. See you at the office," he said with a sympathetic look, and walked to his car.

Laura stood on the sidewalk staring after him, wondering how she could have been so blind.

The Knots Landing Police Station's computer room was crowded and noisy when Sid met his lawyer to run through the list of license plates.

They stood before a glowing computer screen while an operator punched in data.

"I sure hope this does it," Sid said.

"You and me both." Loesser grew quiet as various descriptions of vans began flashing onto the screen. All began with the license plate "I-C-K."

"Could you put that last one back on?" Sid asked suddenly. It glowed before his eyes. "Sorry, I'm mistaken."

"That's okay. We've got all day." Loesser

slapped Sid's back. "This system covers only registrations of northeastern L.A. County."

"Great. How many are there?" Sid asked, as the descriptions kept coming.

"Shouldn't be more than a hundred. If you find one that matches the van you and your wife saw, let me know. I'll be back in an hour or so. Got some running around to do."

"See you then," Sid said, and returned to the screen.

When Loesser returned, he looked over the computer print-out. "Anything?"

"No," Sid said, rubbing his eyes. "I need a breather, Stan."

"Okay, that's enough for now."

The computer operator halted the flow of information with the touch of a button.

"I got a print-out here of all the vans' registered owners," he said. "I was scanning it and saw a familiar name—Rodney Williams."

"Means nothing to me," Sid admitted.

"Pam's police report shows that she was arrested for petty theft a year ago with Rodney Williams."

Sid smiled. "So you think they know each other?"

"They were partners. They stole merchandise all over town until they were finally caught. There's no doubt that Pam knows Rodney Williams."

"Which one of these vans is his?" Sid asked.

Stan stared at the sheaf of papers, then

at Sid. They eagerly went to work.

Karen drove quickly through the back streets of downtown Knots Landing. Beside her, Abby fumbled with a Polaroid camera.

"Is it loaded?" Karen asked.

"I guess." Abby poised her finger above the shutter button. "Let's find out." A click later, a small white photograph spewed out the front of the camera.

Karen grinned.

"I still don't understand. Pam was arrested with this guy who owns the van. So what? She doesn't even say there was a van."

"I know," Karen said. "But maybe there's a way to prove the van was there."

"How?"

"I don't know. I'm just following orders, like you."

Abby smiled and studied the camera.

Karen turned onto 14th street, checking the street numbers. "It should be just up ahead," she said, and pulled to the curb before a run-down two-story house. Parked in the driveway was an orange and red flame-streaked van.

"That's the van I saw!" She nudged Abby. "Go ahead!"

Abby left the car warily, creeping closer to the van. She looked through the viewfinder and moved her finger to the button.

"Come on!" Karen yelled from the car.

"All right!" She snapped two quick shots and ran to the car.

"Step on it!" Abby said, breathless with excitement. Karen quickly sped away from the house.

"I hope he didn't see us," Abby said, pulling the pictures from the camera. She held one gingerly in each palm, waiting for the pictures to appear.

Karen slowed her speed as they neared the police station. And then before their very eyes, an image of the van appeared in glorious, living color.

Abby winked at her companion. "We did it!" she whispered.

Abby found Officer Ted Bright typing up a report in the inspector's room after she left Karen with Sid and Stan Loesser in the computer room. She smiled as she approached him. "Hello, Officer Bright," she said, staring at the badge pinned to his muscular chest. Not bad, she thought.

He looked up. "Hi," he said. He immediately turned his attention back to his typing. But the image of Abby finally sank in and he looked back up. "Hello!"

She smiled graciously. "I was wondering if you could do me a favor."

"Sure, if I can," Bright said, smiling as he ran his eyes over her.

"It's real simple." Abby leaned over his desk and placed a photograph on top of the officer's typewriter. "That night while you were arresting Sid Fairgate—"

Officer Bright scowled. "Yeah?"

"While you were actually *arresting* him, do

you remember seeing an orange and red van—this one, in fact—drive by?"

He looked at the picture and sighed. "Let me think. Ah, yeah, yeah, I guess so. It went over a bump or something and made a noise. I looked up and saw it."

Abby smiled. "Great. And it was this van?" She tapped the picture.

"Could be. It didn't make much of an impression on me, not with a seventeen-year-old girl screaming rape." He smiled. "You're not disappointed in me, are you?"

Abby shook her head. "No, of course not! But this is a fairly unusual van. Don't you think so?"

"Sure, but there's thousands of vans on the streets. A lot of them are pretty wild-looking."

The woman frowned. "You can't identify this van?"

"Only if it's the only one in the world painted that color, with those flames."

"This is the same van," Abby said. "I know it is. All I have to do is find some proof."

"How do you know it's the same one?" Bright asked.

"I feel it . . . inside," she told him.

"Yeah?" Bright wiped his upper lip. "What's it feel like?"

Abby smirked. "You're the officer who took the girl's statement, right?"

He shook his head. "Sorry, it was Thompson, my partner."

"Do you remember what she said? She

didn't mention a van, did she?"

"No. I know that for a fact," the cop said. "It's on her official statement."

Abby smiled. "But later that night, here at the station, after Sid Fairgate was released, she started screaming, didn't she?"

"Yeah. *Boy*, was she a screamer!"

"And she mentioned the van." Abby held her breath.

"Come to think of it, yeah, she did." His face brightened. "She said something about how Fairgate threatened her, how the men in the van were going to hurt her, or something like that. Yeah, I remember. She definitely mentioned the van once we brought her to the station." He touched the picture. "Is this the van?"

"Yes," Abby said, smiling. Out of the corner of her eye, she noticed Karen entering the room. Abby kept looking at the officer, smiling.

"How are you related to this Fairgate, anyway?" Bright asked.

"I'm his sister—his unmarried sister," she added in a low, sensuous tone. "You will speak to the District Attorney about all this, won't you?"

"Sure," he said. "No sweat." He stared at the beautiful blond woman.

"Listen, Officer Bright—"

"Call me Ted." He smiled at her encouragingly.

"Well, Ted, what time are you off tonight?"

"Ah, six." Bright's eyes widened in

anticipation, and his face flushed red.

"Okay. Be a good boy until then, and I'll see you at six o'clock." She slipped the picture back into her purse and winked. "Bye!"

He waved after her as Abby walked over to Karen. The two women left the room, tense but unwilling to show their feelings in front of the officers.

"Well?" Karen demanded once they were in the hallway.

"He remembers seeing the van *and* Pam's mentioning it the night Sid got arrested!"

Karen hugged her. "Great! Let's go!" They hurried off to find Sid and Stan.

Karen sat beside Sid in the District Attorney's office less than an hour later. She pushed her hand into his, and Sid clasped it warmly. Beside them stood Stan Loesser.

Across the room, Pam and Selma Messinger sat with their eyes downcast. They were clearly unhappy at being called to the D.A.'s office on such short notice.

"So after hearing all this new evidence, you still say that Sid Fairgate tried to rape you?" The D.A. sat behind his desk, watching the girl closely.

Pam glanced at her mother, who nodded. "Yes," she said.

"Miss Messinger, that's your right. However, as State Representative, and your representative, I must warn you that this new information almost completely invalidates your testimony," the D.A. said calmly.

"Hey!" Selma cried. "Wait a minute! I thought you were playing on our team!"

"Legally, I can't hold back any information which comes to my attention that might help the defendant. That's the law."

Pam frowned. "What's the big deal here, anyway? Okay, so I forgot about the van. Big deal. It was just a van—it wasn't Rodney's."

"Are you certain of that?" the D.A. asked.

"Hey, she said it, and she meant it! My daughter doesn't lie!"

The D.A. leaned back in his chair, hands folded on his stomach, looking at the Messingers.

Sid tightened his grip on Karen's hand. She desperately wanted to say something but she didn't dare.

The D.A. pushed a button on his intercom. "Would you have him come in?" he asked his secretary. He turned back to look at the Messingers as they waited out an awkward moment.

Finally the door opened. A shaggy-haired, slender teen-age boy shuffled in, dressed in torn jeans and a stained pullover shirt. He looked calmly at the D.A., then guardedly at Pam.

Pam's composure slipped at the sight of the boy. Selma looked interested.

"Have a seat, Rodney," the D.A. offered.

The boy stared at the chair, realized that it faced Selma and Pam, and shook his head. "No thanks, sir. I'd rather stand." He flicked the hair from his eyes with a snap of his head.

"You know this young woman, don't you?" the District Attorney asked, gesturing toward Pam.

"Sure," Rodney said, and cleared his throat.

"On the night she claims Sid Fairgate attempted to rape her, you were with her, weren't you?"

"Yeah," Rodney said slowly.

"In fact, you're friends with Pam. You used to hang out a lot together, didn't you, Rodney?" the D.A. asked gently.

"Uh-huh."

"Why don't you tell us all what you told me a few minutes ago—how you and Pam figured out a great way to make some money."

Rodney shrugged. "We didn't do it all the time, you know. It was, well, just when we were broke. Or when we had nothing else to do. Pam said it was fun . . . You know, we'd wait on a quiet street until a flashy car drove by. Pam would stick out her thumb."

"Hey! He's lying!" Pam said desperately.

Selma glanced at her daughter, her face concerned.

"No, I'm not. If the guy wouldn't pick her up, I'd, like, pretend to rough Pam up."

"Shut up!" Pam insisted.

"Let him finish," the D.A. told her.

Rodney wiped the sweat from his forehead. "Sometimes the guy'd come back and give her a lift. Then, inside the car, she'd ask for money." Rodney avoided Pam's poisonous stare.

"He's lying," Pam said angrily.

"I'm telling the truth! And if the guy didn't give her any money, she said she'd cry rape."

"He's been paid to say this!" Selma thundered, rising from the chair. "Fairgate's lawyer paid him!"

"Sit down, Mrs. Messinger. Neither the Fairgates nor their lawyer have ever talked to Rodney. They gave me the information and I took it from there."

"Big deal! I don't care if he swears on a stack of bibles! I know what money can buy. He's lying about my daughter!" She turned to Pam. "We're not liars, are we, Pammy?"

Her daughter lowered her gaze, her face expressionless.

Selma's eyes narrowed. "Pam, tell them!"

"Mrs. Messinger," the D.A. began.

Sid released Karen's hand. They looked at each other as Selma continued to rant on about her daughter's innocence.

"As State Representative, I'm recommending that all charges against Sid Fairgate in this matter be dropped immediately due to the plaintiff's perjury."

Sid turned to Karen, his eyes filled with love, life, happiness and freedom. He kissed his wife eagerly. "I can't thank you enough," he said, turning toward Stan Loesser. He shook the man's hand.

Karen turned from her husband and looked at Pam, who was slumped in her chair, biting her lip nervously.

"You can all go now, except for the Messingers," the D.A. said.

Karen, Sid and Stan left the office with Rodney.

"I can't ever thank you enough," Sid said, shaking the boy's hand.

"Don't thank me," he said, glancing over his shoulder. "If I hadn't told them everything, I'd be behind bars by now." He headed off toward the street.

"You still did the right thing!" Karen called out.

"Well, Sid, how's it feel to be a free man again?" Stan asked.

"Wonderful!" Sid glowed. "Incredible!"

"I haven't seen you smile like that in ages," Karen said.

"What'll happen to the girl?" he asked.

Stan shrugged. "Hard to say. That depends on how she acts and what the D.A. decides is the best course of action."

"Will she go to jail?" Karen asked.

"Probably. She's a tough nut to crack. I wonder how many other men she's done this to?"

Karen shivered. "Forget about that, Stan. She won't be doing it again for a while."

"Yeah." Sid wrapped one arm around Karen and the other around Stan. The three of them walked slowly to the parking lot, smiling.

Chapter Eleven
A New Beginning

Outside the District Attorney's office, Selma Messinger stood motionless, staring at the wall. She was numb with shock.

It was unbelievable. She couldn't *believe* that her daughter had lied to her and the entire city. How could Pam have done such a thing?

She glanced across the hallway at Pam. Her daughter stood with her head down and eyes closed. *This time,* Selma thought, *you're in real trouble, and your mother can't get you out of it. But then, you're nearly eighteen—it's time you started growing up.*

Selma began to walk toward her daughter, then stopped. They hadn't exchanged a word since leaving the District Attorney's office a few moments ago. All at once she'd learned that her daughter was lying, that she had tried to trick an innocent man—several innocent men—out of money, and that she'd nearly ruined a man's life because he wouldn't pay her a hundred dollars.

Selma sighed. *I raised you the best I could. It wasn't my fault your father died when you were two, and that I got caught up with that musician who gambled all our money away. I tried to see that you had a good childhood,* she thought desperately.

Pam glanced up at her, then looked away, avoiding her mother's eyes. But in that glance Selma saw all she needed to know. Her daughter was sorry.

She shook her head and walked slowly over to the girl. She stood awkwardly before her, then wrapped Pam in her arms.

"Oh, Mom!" Pam burst into tears.

"I know, honey, I know," Selma said, stroking her hair, forgetting, for the moment, what her daughter had done.

At the front door, Karen turned around and looked down the hall. She saw Selma approach her daughter, then embrace her. Karen frowned. She didn't blame the woman for believing her daughter's lies, but that Pam . . .

She shook her head.

"Are you coming?" Sid asked, holding the door open for her.

"I'm sorry." She smiled. "I was just thinking about Pam."

"I know," Sid said.

Karen breezed through the doors. "Is this the end of it, Stan?"

"Most of it. There are formal procedures to go through, but Sid's off the hook. Permanently."

"Terrific!" Sid couldn't stop smiling.

Karen sighed. "How long before the newspapers and radio believe that? I don't think I can stand to live with these lies any longer."

"There's an easy way to clear that all up," Stan said.

"How?"

"We can talk to the media. Get out the story about Sid's innocence, and the D.A.'s decision, as soon as possible. That's the best way to fight bad press—feed it positive information."

"It makes sense," Sid said, nodding.

"Wait a minute," Karen said. "I don't know. They've been so awful to us."

"Come on, honey. It's the fastest way to clear me, at least in the eyes of the public. I say we go for it. Interviews, pictures, the whole works."

"I was hoping you'd agree with me," Stan said. They walked out the front of the building.

"Why's that?" Karen asked, and turned.

Two unflappable television reporters stood beside their camera and sound crews, while nearby at the base of the steps, more reporters and photographers stood waiting. They moved forward as the doors opened.

As Sid, Stan and Karen descended the steps, they were greeted with questions, flashes and microphones thrust in their faces.

"The District Attorney just dropped all charges against Sid Fairgate," Stan told them. "Pam Messinger was lying, to put it plainly."

"Does that mean that there never was a rape attempt?"

"That's exactly what it means," Sid said. "She called the police when I refused to give her a hundred dollars. She set me up."

"Sid Fairgate is one of the most moral people I've ever met," Stan Loesser said. "The charges were absurd. I'm surprised it took the court this long to see that."

"Mrs. Fairgate, what do you think about Pam Messinger now?" the other reporter asked.

Karen smiled. "I'm trying not to."

The reporter laughed. "And you, Mr. Fairgate?"

Sid paused. "I'm just glad it's all over. I wouldn't want anyone to go through what I've been through. As for Pam . . ." He shook his head. "I'll forget I ever heard her name and go on, which is all I can do."

"Would you still pick up a teen-age girl walking the streets at night?" the reporter asked.

"What do you mean, pick up?" Sid asked. "I never pick up young girls. I offered Pam Messinger a ride because I thought she was in trouble. I didn't realize it was part of a scam she had going with two of her friends.

But let me ask you this, sir," Sid said to the reporter. "If you saw a young girl being beaten by a punk on the street at night, wouldn't you stop and offer her a lift?"

"Why, I—"

"You bet your life you would. You wanna know why? Because for every Pam Messinger out there, there are a hundred *good* people. I was brought up to give people a hand, to help them when things get tough. Just because I got into trouble for it this time doesn't mean I won't do it again." He smiled. "You've got a lot of nerve asking me that. Sure, I'll be more careful in the future, but when you make a split decision there's always room for error."

The reporter was silent.

"You know, you're just lucky it wasn't *your* car Pam stopped," Sid said.

Karen took his hand.

Loesser waved the reporters and photographers off.

"I'm proud of you," Karen whispered, squeezing his hand.

"You don't think I was too hard on him, said too much?" Sid asked. "I couldn't help myself. That stupid question!"

"It's okay," Loesser said. "He had it coming to him. Now let's go get a bite to eat. I'm starving!"

On Seaview Circle, Sid stood before his children in the front lawn. "It's over," he said.

"I'm so glad, Daddy!" Diana ran to him, throwing her arms around him.

"That means I won't get beat up anymore?" Michael asked.

Sid smiled. "I can't promise that, but you won't get it because of me. I'm sorry you kids had to weather through this with me, but it's in the past now. Let's just forget it. Okay?"

Eric nodded. "Okay. And Dad, I'm sorry about how I acted."

Sid smiled. "Me too."

Karen smiled, watching from the window.

Laura hurried out of her house, breathless. "Abby!" she yelled.

Abby turned from where she stood before the vacant gray house on the cul-de-sac. Beside her Val was a bundle of nerves, smoothing out her skirt, biting her nails.

"Hope it's good news," Abby said.

Laura smiled proudly. "Abby, it's okay. I arranged everything."

"I can rent the house?" she asked, looking at it.

"Yes."

"But no lease? I don't want to be . . . well, if it doesn't work out with the kids, you know . . ."

Laura smiled. "You can rent it from month to month. You can stay as long or as short as you want."

"That's great!" Abby said.

"Great? It's terrific!" Val clapped her hands together excitedly.

"I told them that Sid's been cleared of all charges, but they said the house will probably be difficult to sell for some time now. People are so picky about where they live—any hint of controversy turns them right off."

Val turned to Abby, her eyes shining. "Maybe someone we know will move in. Maybe *you'll* want to buy it, Abby."

Abby smiled mysteriously. "We'll see," she said sweetly. "You can bet one thing, though—this town will never be the same if I decide to stay!"

Sid and Karen walked up to the trio. At the same moment, Olivia and Brian ran out from Val's house and jumped up and down around Abby, trying to draw her attention. Olivia held the boy's plastic trumpet.

"Mom!" Brian said.

"Mom!" Olivia repeated.

"She took my trumpet!" Brian bellowed.

"She took my trumpet!"

"Olivia, if Brian didn't share his trumpet with you, give it back to him, okay?" Abby asked sweetly.

Olivia shook her head and ran off. Brian followed her. Then Abby turned and joined in the chase. "Olivia!" she yelled.

Karen turned to Sid. "Well, now that this whole thing's over, maybe you can help Abby find some place to live. After all, she is your sister."

"You don't have to," Val said. "She already found a place. Just now."

Sid turned to Laura. "You have anything to do with this?"

She smiled. "Why, Sid, I'm just a secretary in a real estate office. What could I possibly—"

"Where is it?" Karen asked. "Is it far? I'd love to see it."

Laura turned to Val, then smiled. "I wouldn't say it's too far, no. I'd say it was pretty close." Her smile faded as her husband pulled into their driveway. "You tell them, Val. Excuse me." She approached her husband slowly as he left his car. "Hi, Richard," she said, testily. "Guess what?"

No answer.

"Sid's been cleared of everything. All charges were dropped against him." She watched him closely.

Richard looked over at Sid. His eyes were cold and hard . . . almost hateful. There was an awkward moment of silence and then he spoke in a voice loud enough for all of them to hear.

"Well, that sure makes *my* day," he said with a sneer. "He wouldn't stop at anything to get what he wanted—even if it meant walking all over *me*." His eyes narrowed. "He may be out of jail . . . but he can go to hell, for all I care."

"Hey, Richard," Sid began. "Listen, I'm sorry—"

The door slammed shut as the lawyer disappeared into the house.

Laura shrugged helplessly, and hurried in

after her husband, her face flushed.

Karen touched Sid's arm. "I'm sure Richard didn't mean all those awful things. He'll come around eventually."

Sid stared at his neighbor's house, his face darkened with worry. "I don't know, Karen. He can be pretty unforgiving . . . and I've never seen him so angry, so hateful . . ."

"Please, Sid, don't let him spoil this wonderful day . . ."

Just then, Abby reappeared with two children in tow. Brian was holding his shiny trumpet up proudly.

"So, Abby, where's this new house Laura was talking about?" Sid asked, forcing himself to forget Richard—at least for now.

"So, Abby, where's this new house?" Olivia repeated.

Abby glared at her daughter. "The gray one. Right there." She motioned behind her shoulder.

"The gray one. Right there."

"Hey! That's enough of that!" Val said sternly.

"Hey! That's enough . . ." Olivia looked at Val sheepishly and didn't say another word.

"That close? That's wonderful," Sid said. "Isn't it, Karen?"

The woman smiled. "Yes."

"So, Sid," Abby said. "How's it feel to be a celebrity? You're all over the radio, television and newspapers."

"I'll tell you all about it," he said as they walked home, all of them laughing and talking, the two children following.

Once everyone was inside, Karen closed the door firmly. The nightmare was over. No more strange phone calls in the middle of the night, or suspicious looks at the supermarket. No more doubts or fears. No more waiting.

"Karen, honey, are you all right?" Sid asked, at her side.

She looked at him and felt her control begin to slip. "Oh, Sid, I'm fine. Just fine!" Karen fell into the comfort of his arms. At long last, the nightmare was over.

While the crisis was over for Sid and Karen Fairgate, the nightmare was just beginning for the Averys. Richard stared across the street at the Fairgate home and slammed his fist against the wall, bringing a startled Laura to her feet. Smarting over Sid's rejection of his legal advice, Richard took this as just one more blow to his increasingly fragile ego. To make matters worse, Sid had won his case without Richard.

"How dare he embarrass me that way!" Richard's fists came together in a ball of fury. "He had no right to treat me that way!"

Laura cautiously studied her husband. She was confused by his ravings, but dared not ask what he was talking about. Instead, she had learned during times like this to divert his attention and calm him down. Knowing first-hand how vicious Richard could be, Laura wanted to avoid his wrath at all costs.

"Honey, let me fix you something to eat," she offered.

Richard turned on her in a rage. "Why do you do that? I hate it when you patronize me. I would expect that from the noble Sid Fairgate, but not from my own wife!" Richard's eyes were filled with contempt.

Normally, an angry outburst by Richard would chill Laura to her very soul—but not tonight. She was weary. For months she had seen her marriage slowly fall victim to Richard's growing paranoia. Laura increasingly found herself weighing her words to keep him from launching another tirade. Tonight her thoughts crystallized. She had to get out of the house. She yearned for a way to make her mark in the world, not as Richard Avery's wife, but as a sensitive, intelligent individual.

Laura felt her heart sink as she realized that Richard would never approve. His ego wouldn't be able to stand it. But at that moment, watching Richard's irrational tantrum, Laura suddenly didn't care. From this point on, she would be her own person. And Richard would just have to accept it.

But could he?

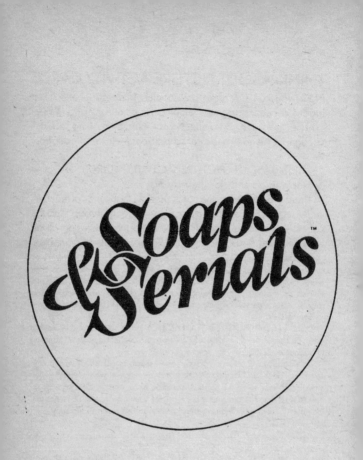